RARE

RARE

A dark anthology of unusual secrets

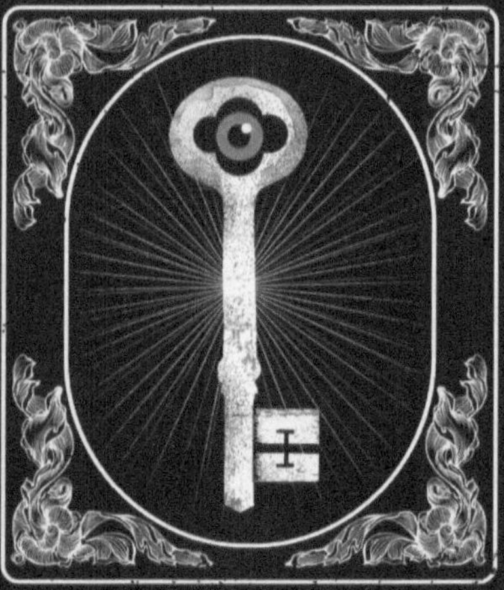

Edited by June Visosky and
Stephanie Vislay

ALEX PARKER PUBLISHING
CALIFORNIA

AN ALEX PARKER PUBLISHING ORIGINAL 2025

To the seekers, the whisperers, and the ones who dare to peer into the
shadows—
This collection is for those who find wonder in the unseen, terror in
the unknown, and revelation in the forgotten corners of the world.
May these stories lead you down winding paths of mystery, through
veils of forbidden knowledge, and into the heart of secrets too rare to
be spoken aloud.
For the ones who listen when others turn away—this book is yours.
— June Visosky

For KANE.
— Stephanie Vislay

CONTENTS

Secrets are lies we keep to ourselves, an alternate reality we delicately craft with light and illusion to obscure who and what we really are. We shape-shift in this artificial glow; we manipulate reality and demand compliance with these hidden truths and concealed desires. Secrets are born out of necessity, and when all goes well, they function as our obedient servants. Left unattended, however, they can turn on us. What was once a small pebble in our shoe becomes a boulder that eventually breaks us.

In *RARE*, authors weave compelling stories of where shadows meet the light. The curtain is pulled back, and a fleeting glimpse of truth alters everything. The stories explore intimate, powerful ways secrets bond and destroy our identities, our relationships, our futures, and our pasts. *RARE* invites you to discover these extraordinary secrets set against the backdrop of the unconventional, the unpredictable, and the unseen.

Journey into worlds unknown and secrets as dark as the characters that hold them. Discover hidden pacts between unlikely companions and tests of will for the unassuming hero. Walk the maze of mirrors as *RARE* conceals, reveals, and unfolds the complexity of human experience. This anthology will leave you questioning what you thought you knew and reaching for answers just beyond your grasp.

Sink into the darkness of *RARE* stories crafted by some of the most creative minds in fiction. We welcome you to take your first step into the labyrinth. But take care not to get lost...

RARE STEAKS
Laura Foley

"**S**peak, man."

I know King Vella is talking to me because who else could it be when the long table of twenty or so chairs is only occupied by us? Him at the top, me at the end, divided by mountains of food. Of grapes and cheese. Bread and various meats woven around an array of slumping candles.

I've been riding all day, and now that night has somehow arrived, the bank of arched, rose-tinted windows lining the high-rise brick appear lackluster without light to shine the stories of the women back at us.

Now, they all look sad despite their beautiful naked bodies against serene backdrops. I twist my wedding ring to remind myself of Fena. My heart aches for her, but I return my hand tightly to lock it around the knife in my pocket instead of massaging the achy feeling out of my chest.

"I am Naev of the Fellwood Region, and when I was a boy . . . " I start, just as I practiced. "I helped my father—"

"No!" Vella barks. Bits of his turkey legs spittled across the table.

"No?" I am a large man, and this word I rarely hear. I keep my gaze firmly on him. Taken aback or not, I will not falter on my intentions tonight.

"Tell me what you want," the king demands. "No silly story. Just tell me why you are worth the Balor Opal I accepted to meet with you. Why did you give away such a great fortune on behalf of Queen Larna to deliver this message? Allyship? Mercy?"

His impatience stills me. To know of a man, then to meet him, creates a divot in understanding who they truly are. I know he is evil. That he holds no mercy to plead with or barter opals with. But seeing his piggery and lack of charisma through the eyes of this lowly messenger quells the slight tickle of nerves I carried with me as I walked into this grand hall. This hall with sparkling chandeliers with wheels of candles, with golden cutlery for empty guests.

I clear my throat. "'It must end'—that is the message I was sent here to tell you."

The king attempts to spin the many rings on his fingers now too welded on over time to move. His oafish demeanor no doubt still draws a legion of women to his bedchamber at night. And to what end? I guessed nought of him works well these days, or rather, these nights. The wine he slugged on certainly helped little. There was surely more chance of the sourdough baguettes fulfilling those women than his limp counterpart.

"No," King Vella bellows before heaving so many olives into his mouth their juices dribble down his bearded chin.

"No?" I repeat, shifting in my seat to sit higher. Is that all he had to say? I want to ask for the opal back. Return to its rightful land. Or sell it on to the highest bidder and at least return home with carriages of food for the final days. Then again, maybe death by hunger was preferred over that of the sword of Vella's men. Because they would come. They *had* come already.

Vella's stare is fixed on his plate. I am but an inconvenience, which I suppose I knew before ever entering these halls, but I need more time. "You may leave now."

I stare at one of the women painted onto the window again. Each gentle stroke of the artist's brush was thoughtful. The one in the middle is careening her body over the rocks of a quiet coastline.

It can't be comfortable. Lying over jagged rocks like that. I pity her. She is but the desire of men, no one cares if her bones ache. If she longs to swim in the sea. If she is the one who wishes to paint.

Fena, I think again. Beautiful Fena with her midnight hair and green eyes. How her love for me was always whispered. She could not paint, but she could sow and fletch arrows, and sing lilting lullabies.

I need to do this for Fena. For our boy. Our girl.

I clench my eyes and take a deep breath.

"Can I eat before I go?" I ask, uncaring of the hunger certainly clear in my eyes. In the sunken, purple circles around them.

The king laughs, bellowing into the hall so fiercely the heads of the candles struggle to stay alight.

The two guards at the door exchange a shifting glance, the *ting* of their heavy armor ringing for a moment.

Shimmying in his groaning chair, King Vella grins and wags a finger at me like I've done enough to break through his barrier of boredom or, perhaps, apathy. "I tell you what, each time you take a piece of food and eat it, you can move up a chair in the row. And if you reach me, you end the war." He laughs and claps his hand as though he's impressed by his own idea. "You can kill me with that knife you've been toying with in your pocket since you arrived."

I clench it harder.

It matters not that he knows I snuck it in now.

"No one can keep a secret from me. I may be fat and old, but I never lost my wits from days on the battlefield. I was near your size, a big fellow. The Stag, my brethren called me. So, what do you say? Shall you play the game?"

"Hardly seems fair," I say to force his hand. There is more to this.

He scoffs, hocking up a food I didn't care to know of. "What is not fair is expecting an equal world when the kings provide rule and the poor provide nothing. Now listen, and listen well. If I provide you a meal it comes with a stake."

I nod. What other choice to have?

"Alright. I accept your offer, King Vella."

"If you reach the final seat, you kill me, yes? That is what we agree. Alas, if you do not succeed, then come morning, I will take your village and wipe it clean until it is a barren land." The king's fingers interlink. "Now, do you wish to continue?"

Answering his question again, I lean forward and rip a tiny piece of cheddar off its skewer, popping it into my mouth with a quick throw. My stomach tightens, instinctively prepared for the trick of it being poisoned. Instead, I'm so shaken by its beautiful, rich flavor, I find my hand grasping the chair's arm to mask my joy.

"Wonderful." The king claps again. "I must tell you before we go any further. Just before midday, an employee of the palace was caught sending messages to my latest wife. Disgusting messages. I am told they are in love—which matters not to me—but to expect to deceive a king and escape with no punishment?" He barks another laugh. "Foolish. Now, why do I tell you this?"

I merely shrug.

"He was my taster. The man who ensures there are no poisonous goods among the pile. He had the smell and sense of a hound. Tis a pity with this one, though. He only lasted six months before we strung up his head on the front wall earlier today. It must be a record. All this to say, I have elected you as my taster tonight."

The king smirks.

I swallow my reaction.

"But you ate the olives," I gently protest. "A man who lives on the edge of death?"

"No. A man who grows his own olives. Now, eat."

Taking my rightful seat in the first of the line after surviving the cheese, I opt next for the sourdough, slightly burnt on its edges, a flower cut into crust. Breaking it in half, I place it down on the prepared plate and take a large, warm bite. Embarrassed by how beautiful it tastes, I cover my nose with my fist to stifle the deep inhales I can't seem to control. It seems I've been starving for so long, I've forgotten: food, poisoned or not, is delicious.

The ritual goes on this way over and over. And the feeling of chance grows smaller and smaller as I begin to indulge in the meats and yellow fruits. The garlic potatoes. The rosemary stuffing.

The king fills his cup of red wine twice by his own hand—a reckless act.

Now, we are merely two seats divided. Perhaps he thought I'd fall down by the fourth chair. Perhaps the excitement has grown thin on the gluttonous royal with how everything quickly went. Perhaps it is simply past his bedtime.

"Your next choice?" he asks, displaying the table of endless goods to me.

I scan the food meticulously, then clutch two slivers of beet between my fingers. Its purple stains them, seeping into the worn prints. Fena used to foretell my future with the lines when we lay in bed at night. She promised good things for us, but yet never did see this night.

A dangerous gurgle ripples throughout my stomach, echoing the room. I dare say I am getting full, no longer attuned to the stretch my stomach once knew. The beet is bitter and earthy, swallowed in two bites. Another gurgle catches in my side. I clutch it quickly, growing weary of this unbeatable game.

"I shall pick the final food," the king declares.

I shoot him with a firm side eye. "You break your own rules?"

"I am the king! I make and break and amend rules every day of my life. This is no different."

Coward.

Attempting to untangle the knots in my rigid jaw to no joy, I manage a silent nod.

The final meal: a steak.

Using a large, two-pronged meat fork, he plops it onto my plate with an oafish wheeze. A meat of three inches in height. It would have fed my entire family.

"On with it, then."

Drawing the knife from my pocket, I smirk at the king. The two guards, hands on hilts, become hostile behind me.

King Vella settles them with a mere wave of his hand. "It is an honour to feast on a beautiful, rare cut. If the man wishes to carve his own meat. Leave him."

In their retreat, I begin to cut, tearing it from itself, the tendons soft, the meat red and uncooked entirely beneath its seared surface.

"Just shipped in this week from Henshal Island. A prize cow, I'm told. You've heard of Henshal Island? Among our most loyal followers. They pledged allegiance at the beginning of the war and have been rewarded as such. They provide ten cows and ten women every week and we leave them to their island lands in peace."

"Why give me a final meal if you have confidence it holds no poison? That those farmers are loyal?" The fork with a piece of the dripping meat rests a fraction from my lips.

The king shrugs.

I take the bite. Chewing it several times.

"I must say," the king says, interrupting my chewing. "I should mention, the man—my taster—his brother is my butcher. We import the meat whole."

My chewing draws the meat to stasis in my mouth. I look at him out of the corner of my eye. He's grinning, all his rotten teeth on display. This, *this* is what brings him joy. To catch even the simplest of messengers out. To delight in the moment a man realizes he is dead, no matter if breath still fills his lungs, or scraps of hope still run through his mind.

"Merassah."

"What?" The king says. "Speak up, boy."

Boy. I have not been named a boy since I buried my mother as a child.

I swallow the piece of meat, swallow forcefully, so he can see it slide past my Adam's apple. "Merassah—the butcher. That is his name."

The king dashes a glance at one of his footmen by the door. I do not need to turn to see his answer, for I know he is nodding.

"How did you know?" Vella asks, aghast.

It is me laughing now, a thing I did not know I could do anymore. "King Vella, you were so busy taking over the country you forget how united we have been forced to become. I know what food was tainted with poison because grapes that size only grow in Glasbán, and you murdered their fourteen-year-old king on his inauguration day. His mother wept so loud, she coughed up blood. I know that those tiny tomatoes only thrive in the northern heat of Louthford where you took the hands of sixteen children before their first birthday. I knew every poisoned food because they were *sent* to you poisoned. It has been weeks of preparation. The only foods safe to eat were the ones grown locally, by people you could trust: the potatoes, the corn, the food that could thrive in the harsh weather here. It is all an act with you, I knew this when I saw the golden doors to this room. The chandeliers. The rose-tinted windows. This table, full of food you cannot even touch to your lips."

"Guards."

I use my knife to take the first out before he moves an inch. The knife skims across the room, darting into his throat's center. A wide-eyed gasp, a stifled gurgle, and it's over. The next comes for me, his sword drawn. I stand and the chair thuds to the ground. With a violent swing towards my chest, I pivot, throwing the bowl of pepper into his eyes before grasping his neck from behind, easily locking him into place. Unhitching his pencil dagger from his belt, two stabs to his side—between the second and third rib as my father taught me—and his lungs are failing. I offer a third strike to his center, dragging it upwards. The man, unable to breathe from the first punctures, stifles a groan before the limpness of him brings enough satisfaction in me to release him to the ground.

The king staggers back, unable to shimmy out of his throne chair without the aid of his staff.

"You thought the secret was yours, but what makes a secret rare—rarer than this steak—is the ability for an *entire*, frightened country to keep it from the one man who tried to destroy it. You say the stakes are rare here. I agree. For it is the life of one man risked for an entire country to live."

"I am no man. I am a king!"

I pace to him, my voice thunderous. "I am the man in this story! I am the man of this story because you are nothing. They will remember nothing of you, tyrant, apart from perhaps the title of the 'Foolish King'. The king who allowed his greatest enemy to walk right into his halls and share a meal with him."

I am the tiresome one now. The one who does not need to drag this misery out.

Taking the guard's unsoiled sword from the ground, I test its weight before quickly plunging it into the king's chest.

A disgusting, groaning gurgle seeps from his mouth. The smell of his insides leaving him to soil his pants cannot be concealed by even the most beautiful smell of food the table has to offer.

I twist the sword, letting it pierce through his back as I take a step closer.

"I am Naev of the Fellwood Region, and when I was a boy," I start, "I helped my father bury my mother just beyond the border of our maize fields. He sealed her stomach back together with her own intestine so she could travel out to the forever lands of Tannor with her body intact. And when I was a man, I had no father to help me bury my wife, nor what was left of my children. I had a shovel. I had my hands, and I had a seed of anger. I threw the seed into the grave with them. My wife, Fena. My daughter, Neasa. My son, who did not get a name because he was three days old when your men came, but who I named Luan after my father because it means *warrior*. That is our line. That is what you stole from me."

I retract the sword, and his body slumps onto the chair, still staring at me.

"If there is anything left of you at this point, and you're wondering why I threw the seed in when I might need anger to get me to this point, it is because I do not want or need to feel anything. I have delivered my message and I have won."

My attention drifts upward just as the morning light breaks through the rose-tinted glass, bathing the beautiful auburn-haired woman in its glow. Her eyes embed mine like she is sending a message from my wife to come home. To find the forever lands of Tannor by my own hands.

"Gladly," I say.

I will go there now, gladly.

Raising the king's steak knife to my throat, I rip its jagged steel across my neck, letting all the bottled torture of my life pour out onto his marble floor until I join it there, at peace knowing revenge is dish best served rare, and the secret of the nation prevailed.

ALONE / TOGETHER
Adam Bassett

Above the haze of city lights, the sky was black and starless. Carl knew there was more out there than he could see, but knowing such things didn't change the empty void outside his bedroom window.

He stood, careful not to wake his wife, and walked to the kitchen, only to remember the fridge was barren. Carl considered the whiskey, then thought better of it, and poured himself a cup of water. It tasted *off*. He left it half-empty on the counter.

He found his sleeping pills in the spare room on top of a hand-me-down dresser. He and Sayra received it as a gift from a neighbor after Sayra became pregnant. It was heavy—made of real wood—with large, white knobs. It was scuffed and dented, worn by years of use. A can of varnish sat beside it on the floor, unopened. A wide paintbrush, still new, rested atop its cover.

Carl glared at the bottle of sleeping pills. They expired a year ago. The instructions called for one; he took two and swallowed. They went down hard.

He stood there a moment, staring at that dresser.

Inside the drawers there was nothing but air.

***

Sayra considered getting out of bed, but the very idea made her stomach turn. As if her body hadn't already betrayed her enough. She spent another morning mulling over what had happened, amazed at how quickly she'd run out of options.

She felt she was the only person without any left.

The blind purchased new eyes. Amputees received limbs. All manner of cables could help people interface with any network under the sun for work, pleasure, or anything else. And those were just the utilities. Cozmods had come a long way in recent years, adapting to new markets wanting to shed a bit of their humanity in favor of something more stylish. A woman could implant lights beneath her skin that changed color on a whim, or dye her body green and replace her vocal cords for a better pair. In the last twenty years, the music industry had split down the middle—one half seeking the perfect sound, the other contracting only natural voices.

Sayra had gotten caught up in all of that, even here in the mountains.

She'd arrived when the waves began to lap up against the Sunrise Highway, just blocks from where she grew up in Massapequa. They'd said that was the furthest the oceans would rise, but it was underwater now. Only by an inch, but that was enough to turn the place into a ghost town.

New York City was fine, though. They'd walled it off years ago. No money was left in the budget for the rest of Long Island, apparently.

Tech could fix someone's most severe ailments, make them look or sound however they wanted, and even hold back oceans so people in cities could go about their lives as though nothing had changed—when they wanted to, anyway.

But where were the advancements for mothers? Why was it that people could be reconstructed practically from scratch, and yet there was an empty room just across the hall? An empty room with an empty crib and an empty dresser for somebody who never got to live a day of their life.

It was all too much.

Too cruel.

Carl tried to rouse her at some point. She pretended to be asleep, and he let her be. Sayra knew her husband meant well, and that he was hurting, too, but she couldn't get up, and she couldn't console him. Sayra didn't have it in herself to even try. She just needed to rest, but doing so weighed her down with guilt. Speaking with her husband *should* be within her reach. She *should* be able to eat without having to starve herself first. Instead, she was making him go through this alone. She loved him for helping her and hated herself for not being able to do more. Do *anything*.

The half dozen missed calls from her friends and family only made it worse. Jen had tried again only hours ago. Sayra was glad that Jen hadn't given up on her, even though she absolutely should have. *Sayra* would have.

She needed it to end.

A part of her knew that was a dangerous thought, one that was best untouched, but it came back to her every time she tried to open her eyes.

There were several therapists in the city, as well as doctors who advocated a short list of vaguely familiar medications. Sayra blinked through a list on her lens, a thin device that sat on her eye and displayed information in augmented reality. Doctors' names and biographies floated over her view of the window, its dark curtains drawn over the afternoon sun.

She always found something to critique. The doctor was too far, too expensive, or her insurance didn't cover her visit. The medication was too severe, had terrible side effects, or only concealed the darkness that threatened to swallow her from morning to night. She didn't need it hidden, she needed it gone.

It wasn't until midafternoon—after she refused lunch again—that Sayra found something that looked promising: Recollections LLC. The dark blue logo flickered against the curtains. The company was new in town, but she recognized the name from Long Island. There wasn't a lot of information on her lens, but she recalled some aunts and uncles talking about how their surgeons removed the memories of the floods and helped them move on with their lives.

It was just enough to get her out of bed. Sayra dressed in some clothes that had been lying on the floor and found her bus pass beside them.

Carl asked where she was going. She wasn't sure she wanted to talk to him about it yet, so she said she was going out for some air, which wasn't entirely untrue. She'd been in the house for a week. It would probably be good to walk around the city a bit.

"Oh," he said. "Great. Do you want some company?"

"I don't think so. I just need some time."

"Okay." He nodded. Whether or not he understood the sentiment, she couldn't tell. "I'm going to go pick up a few things then, I think. We're low on water and out of food. Anything you want?"

"No," Sayra said. She paused in the doorway, staring down the long metal staircase. "Whatever you get will be fine."

Sayra left the building, exiting beside the old brick diner. The apartment she shared with Carl had been built on top of it a few years ago as part of a larger housing project that saw the new city rise on the bones of the old. The whole street looked like that: old wood or brick buildings, some built centuries ago, topped with cookie-cutter apartments. Some stretched four or five stories high, battling the trees for sunlight.

She walked a few blocks to the bus stop. It was a small, enclosed space with an ancient wooden bench inside, littered with paper flyers advertising community plays, craft shows, and a missing cat named Suki.

The bus arrived a few minutes later. It seemed too wide for the narrow roads, as if it might catch a mailbox or passing vehicle at any moment, yet the driver was at ease. He leaned back and cast Sayra a glance as she climbed aboard.

"Afternoon," he said as Sayra found a seat.

The old faux leather was cool to the touch and tearing at the seams.

***

Carl meditated on the mundane act of existing in a grocery store, his cart pulled off to the side in aisle three beside the soy sauce. There were twelve kinds to pick from. Some were dark, others tamari, and some had no label at all other than *soy sauce*. Most of the labels were in English. A few were in Japanese. An ad appeared on his lens offering to translate the text if he upgraded to the premium plan. He dismissed it and tossed a bottle into the cart.

He liked the dragon illustration along the label.

These were the little moments of control he'd been missing. That was the thesis of his grocery-based meditation, he decided. That was why he was using the sleeping pills and why he'd put so much energy into trying to help his wife—not that he needed a reason to help Sayra during such a traumatic time, but it felt good to have an explanation for things. The same way it felt good to be making simple, boring decisions again. It didn't matter what kind of soy sauce he got. Neither of them would notice a difference.

After being cooped up at home—after everything he and Sayra had been through—it felt like things were finally inching their way back to normal, whatever that meant now.

***

Sayra opened her eyes just as a flashing light faded away. A headache split through her skull in its wake.

She sat in the maw of a machine that enveloped her head, its arms unfolding and revealing her to the world now that its work was done. She knew what the device was and what it did, but the memory of how she got there was gone.

"How're you feeling, Mrs. Camirin?" the doctor asked. He was dressed in a simple lab coat. Chrome folded all around his eyes, head, and arms. The tech was reminiscent of the mods she and Carl—and most other people—had installed. However, where they had simple slots to import and export data on the side of their heads, the doctor looked like he had crawled out of a science fiction film. His eyes were covered by a complex visor that seemed too large for his body, the name *Recollections LLC* debossed between the lights where his eyes should have been. Cables ran from his temples and the base of his skull into the machine that Sayra sat in, bright blue and green lights illuminating his hair and shoulders.

Sayra grunted in response and turned away from the lights.

"Of course," the doctor said. "Here, take these pills. You'd think after all these years I'd stop asking stupid questions! No, take two. They'll ease the pain. The next twenty-four hours are crucial, Mrs. Camirin. Do not stress yourself. Relax. Rest, and come morning, you'll be feeling much better. Oh, and when you leave, best to go the back way. Protesters out front won't be kind to that headache. Or wait them out in the lobby. There's usually room somewhere."

"Thank you," Sayra said, a bit uncertain what she was thanking the doctor for, but then—that just meant the operation had been successful. The spidery machine had removed a memory.

When she left the operating room, Sayra expected Carl to be waiting for her, but she didn't recognize anyone in the waiting room. A receptionist got Sayra's attention and slid a small black case across the counter. It contained a flash drive, the kind that could easily slot into the reader in her head.

"Your discarded memories are the property of Recollections LLC, but if you need a peek at what you removed just pop that in," he said. "You don't have to look at it if you don't want to—not everyone likes to know why they came to us—but it's there if you want to."

"Thanks," Sayra said, sliding the thin black case into her coat pocket.

"Just don't come back asking to remove the memory of reading it," the receptionist continued, his attention diverted by something on his lens. A flash of red flitted over his eyes. "Removing a memory doesn't work so well the second time. The company avoids it as much as it can. So, if you decide to look, you'll have to live with whatever you see there."

Sayra took a deep breath. She felt as though she'd been handed a live grenade. The pin was still in, but it seemed too feeble a way to prevent an explosion.

"Thanks," she said again.

Sayra walked out through the back door. The protesters were out in full force, chanting, "Our memories are not for sale!" and "Corponauts, corpo-not!" Between that and the traffic, she could feel the migraine getting worse.

As she made her way toward the bus stop, a pit grew in Sayra's stomach. What had been so bad that she needed to remove the memory of it? Was it something she'd done to herself? Had somebody hurt her, or had it been an accident? Sayra trusted she must have had her reasons.

Carl always made fun of her for needing to think every little decision through, yet she was leaving Recollections clutching her memories in her pocket. She didn't know if she could even talk to her husband about it. He hadn't come to pick her up, which suggested he didn't know what she'd done. That made two of them, she supposed.

Or, Sayra wondered, was the memory of something that happened to *him*? She thought back to the last few weeks and could remember glimpses of her life with Carl: eating dinner together and him waking her up to go to the bathroom at night. Nothing stuck out as unusual. Nothing was out of the ordinary.

Carl was probably fine, but she still wondered about his absence. That was unlike him. When they started trying to conceive, he went with her to every consultation, even when she insisted he didn't have to. When his niece was in the hospital, he spent his lunch breaks visiting and playing cards with her.

As she arrived at the bus stop, Sayra decided to keep whatever had happened a secret, at least until she knew more. If she ever learned more. She ran a finger along the edge of the flash drive's case, tempted to slot it in and see what she'd erased, but she couldn't bring herself to do it. Certainly not in public.

Instead, she stood in silence, listening to the autumn wind.

***

Carl was glad to see Sayra on her feet and getting out of the apartment again. She'd spent too much time cooped up since the miscarriage. Both of them had. She looked tired as she left the restroom, but that made sense, given all that she'd been through lately.

"What do I smell?" Sayra asked.

"Dinner," he said, watching her closely as she walked into the kitchen.

"Thank God. I'm starving."

It wasn't anything special, but the stir fry tasted good. He'd mixed some thinly-sliced chicken with carrots, rice, and bell peppers. Over it, he spread soy sauce and synthetic honey with a few spices blended in. An old recipe, and an easy one to make, but it always tasted good.

"Where did you go on your walk today?" he asked as they sat down together.

She shrugged the question off. "Nowhere. Around the block. Lost track of time, or I would have been home sooner."

Carl knew she was lying. If that was all that had happened, she wouldn't have been so dismissive. Under normal circumstances, she would have spent the next half hour talking about her day, detailing all the things she'd seen or heard or learned.

Her response wouldn't have worried him if they hadn't already been through so much that week. If she wanted to keep something to herself, that was fine, but she always told him when she was doing that. She said those things were for her. She would have said something else, like "I don't want to talk about it."

But Sayra didn't say what happened that day was for her alone. She wasn't just keeping something for herself; she didn't want *him* to know she was keeping something secret.

"What about you? How was your day?" she asked.

"It was good," he said. "It felt good to get out of the place, even for just a bit."

Carl noticed she didn't react to the idea of needing to get out of the apartment. Was that a question, somewhere crinkled into her brow? Had he misspoken?

"I stopped by the lake before I came home," he added. "It was quiet."

She sat back in her chair and took a drink from the bottle of soda they were sharing. "I'm surprised. Usually the leaf peepers are all over the place this time of year."

"Probably out east already, jamming up traffic in the mountains."

She chuckled.

Something was definitely wrong.

Since Carl had made dinner, Sayra offered to clean up. That was fairly normal, but again, he was taken aback. She'd been in bed for practically a week straight, ignoring calls from family, friends, and coworkers alike. She'd barely spoken to him. This evening, she was eating with him, laughing, and volunteering to help around the apartment.

Carl heard Sayra turn on the speaker in the kitchen. She asked it to play music by LyttleCafé, and the apartment was filled with the dulcet sounds of Ella Caby and her nylon 6 string. A classic. One of Sayra's favorites. It was like she was back to her old self.

Carl went into the kitchen under the pretense of getting a bottle of water, keen to check on his wife again. She gave him a kiss on the cheek as he passed by her in the narrow kitchen, humming along to Ella's latest album as he left.

He set the bottle down and went to the restroom. While he sat on the toilet, he ran a quick search for rapid recoveries from psychological trauma and post miscarriage depression. Nothing gave him any answers. He was probably searching for the wrong things, but what was he supposed to call whatever *this* was?

It was getting late. Carl washed up, groaning at how the mirror revealed dark circles under his eyes, and ran some floss through his teeth. As he threw it away, he caught sight of something in the trash—an unusual shape next to the usual mess. It was a small black box with a logo across one side: *Recollections LLC.*

Carl's stomach dropped. He picked the box out of the trash and ran numb fingers along the edge. A small flash drive—a black shard made to fit into the port in most personal readers—was housed in it. He pushed it into the slot on the side of his head and the Recollections logo appeared on his lens. Red text appeared over his view of the restroom wall. Below it was a file titled *RBC-Patient_Report-108E2L.*

He opened it, and paragraphs of red text streamed across his view of the bathroom wall.

Carl ejected the flash and threw it back into the trash. He stood there for a moment, breathing slowly, listening to Sayra's music muffled through the door.

A lone guitar plucking. A woman's voice rising and falling with the chorus.

When the songs changed, he went back to the kitchen and poured himself a glass of whiskey.

"Really?" Sayra asked, mirth in her voice.

"Water didn't quite hit the spot," he said, which wasn't entirely untrue.

The whiskey tasted bitter after having just brushed his teeth. His gums stung from the alcohol.

***

Sayra knew something was wrong. The way Carl spoke to her so delicately, treating her like she was about to break, was unnerving.

After she was done with the dishes, Sayra stayed in the kitchen a moment longer, staring at the arrangement of still-drying plates, pots, and utensils while she skimmed through old messages saved to her lens. Red text rolled across her field of vision—weeks-old messages between Carl and herself. She was looking for answers, knowing she probably wouldn't like what she found, but not quite ready to fish through the trash. She didn't need the full picture, just a better idea of what had put her husband so off-balance.

She had deleted most of her recent messages, probably not by accident. Those that remained were simple, like Carl asking if she needed anything or telling her that a shower would help her feel better. At some point, he seemed to have given up with words and sent cat videos. They were adorable, but unhelpful.

Sayra tried the obituaries next, wondering if somebody had died, but she didn't recognize any of the names listed. She checked her bank account to see if she'd suddenly lost some money, but again, there was nothing out of the ordinary.

She wasn't looking in the right places, but she didn't know where to check next. Besides that, Sayra had enough trust in herself to know she would not have removed a memory on a whim. Perhaps she was just overthinking things. Best to move on. Let the past be the past, whatever it was, right?

Carl was on the couch nursing his whiskey and staring out through the window at the mountains beyond. Bags hung beneath his eyes. She hadn't caught that while they were eating together. He'd been so attentive, but just then, as he gazed off into the night sky, she felt as though she was finally seeing his true state of mind.

Sayra joined him on the couch and kissed him, her lips lingering on his a moment longer than usual, testing the waters. His lips curled into a slight grin, but his eyes still looked like they were off in the mountains.

The last time Carl had looked that way was when his niece died. She was only a teenager. She'd gone home, back across the lake, and got caught in a crossfire between police and some gang. A week later, Sayra and Carl were listening to her eulogy.

The wake was short. The body was hidden under a closed casket. Sayra learned from the girl's mother that it was because they had to save money on the service. The burial, the tombstone, the hosting family—it was all so expensive. However, a corpse's chrome still held value so long as it was undamaged. Whatever was under the lid of that girl's casket was a broken, disassembled young woman. Consequently, nobody wanted to show her face to the mourning family.

She knew that Carl knew that. The moment he saw the closed casket, he knew.

Sayra sat back on the couch and brought her husband's head to rest onto her chest. He lay there for a long while, the warmth of his cheek against her. She ran her fingers through his hair. Slowly. Gently. Her fingertips brushed against the chrome in his head. His hair was thinning more than she had realized, but she didn't mind. She thought that old men looked wise—which was totally unfair as far as she was concerned—but she was not afraid of age. She looked forward to growing old with Carl.

That was why they were trying for a baby, after all.

To grow old together.

As a family.

***

Carl lay against Sayra for a while, her arm draped over him like a weighted blanket. He could hear her heart beating steadily. He felt safe and lost all at once. He had his wife back, but she was fundamentally not the woman who woke up in his bed that morning.

Was that a bad thing? She'd barely been able to get out of bed since the miscarriage. Their child's death...it had destroyed her.

She wasn't in pain anymore. She was back to the way she was before it all went awry. So, why wasn't he happier? This was what he'd wished for, prayed for, when she was asleep.

Carl wanted another drink of whiskey, but he couldn't bear to loosen himself from Sayra's grip, so he sat still until he began to doze off. Eventually, she nudged him upright and told him they should go to bed.

Carl didn't bother to take his clothes off. He collapsed on his side of the bed and closed his eyes. He could feel Sayra's stare. She was probably confused and scared, trying to piece together what memories were taken from her. He felt sorry for her.

On the other hand, he didn't know what to say. Telling her what she'd done...that would be worse, wouldn't it? She'd removed those memories for a reason.

"I'm going to stay up a bit longer," she said. Then he heard their bedroom door close.

***

Sayra had never felt so alone. Not with Carl, at least. He'd been a constant in her life since they met, always eager to be at her side, and she'd tried to be the same for him. She'd imagined her marriage immune to the issues of her friends' and family's. Those that withered and grew more distant were not like what they had. Carl wasn't always exciting, for certain. His idea of a good time was watching a show, walking around the neighborhood. Fishing in the mountains on a long weekend–even though he knew there were practically no fish left in the lake and he was legally required to release whatever he caught. But she couldn't imagine another life for herself. Carl was always there, always asking interesting questions, and always supporting her.

There was only one thing left to do.

Sayra dug through the trash. She found the case from Recollections and popped it open. A shiver ran up her spine. The flash drive was missing.

Carl had found it.

Sayra dug deeper into the bin, past the used floss and tissues, and came up with the tiny metal stick after a few minutes.

She wiped it against her jeans and slotted it in, bracing for the worst.

***

The next morning, Carl found Sayra asleep on the couch. He picked up his keys and put on a coat, careful not to wake her, and left the apartment. The sun had yet to rise, but as he drove into South Burlington, it crept up over the Green Mountains and reflected off the lake. Without it, the breeze cut through him like ice.

He arrived at Recollections a few minutes before the doors opened. It was a surprisingly small office set on the bottom two floors of a larger building. The base of the structure looked as old as the city, with cracks in the bricks and gaps in the mortar that kept it all together. The apartments above were new, added sometime in the last thirty years during the worst of the population boom—when refugees fled the flooded east coast.

A handful of protesters began to show up, carrying large signs, greeting each other as if they were old friends just casually meeting up at the park. They'd been at it so long that the news cycle had moved on. Those who remained were the loudest, but there were only four on the sidewalk. Perhaps more would show up as the day warmed up.

When the doors to Recollections opened, Carl still hadn't gotten out of his car. He watched traffic slowly increase as people went to work or drove to the store, and he wondered if he really wanted to do what he was planning. Rather, he didn't *want* to. He wondered if he *should*.

He wished Sayra had talked about it with him. They could have had the operation together or found another way to work through it. Whatever they decided, at least neither of them would have had to be alone.

Now he was doing the same thing to her, although it was different this time. She wouldn't even notice the change, not like he did. She'd already erased those memories.

Carl thought about putting the car into drive, but he couldn't bear another day like the previous one. He couldn't speak with Sayra as she was now. Not with all of his memories of what had happened. He was terrified of invalidating what she'd done by telling her what she'd forgotten. If she thought removing the memories was the best thing to do, maybe it was. Maybe that was what they needed: a restart.

Carl averted his eyes from the protesters as he walked into Recollections. A tech guided him into the operating room, and the doctor described the procedure. He showed Carl the chair that would remove the memories, explaining the process in detail.

After writing down Sayra's name and number in case there was an emergency, Carl answered a slew of basic questions: did he have any allergies, combat implants, malware, history of dementia in the family? He signed his name on a paper that gave Recollections immunity should something go wrong, and acknowledged that the removed memories became property of Recollections LLC and its subsidiaries. Finally, Carl described the situation and the memories he wanted removed, in as much detail as he could.

A call interrupted them. Carl looked at his phone long enough to see Sayra's name, then put it back into his pocket.

"I can wait if you need to take that," the doctor said, the lights in his visor gleaming.

"No. I'll call her back after."

"The procedure takes a few hours. The part where you're sitting in the chair and that little crown does its work is just a part of it—we also need to make sure you're able to walk back out through those doors, which is another matter. We're not just cutters. We gotta put you back together afterward too. And—"

"It's fine," Carl said as he sat in the chair. It seemed to know he was there; the arms around his head flinched when he sat back.

Meanwhile, the doctor connected Carl to the chair via a physical jack in the side of his head and another in a port on his arm. He complained quietly about out-of-date chrome as a series of graphs appeared on a screen, his vitals, on another, Carl could see his heart beating—one hundred forty-two beats per minute—and felt his chest tightening.

White light flashed, and the doctor's eyes became red—a feed of data streaming across his lenses.

"Let's just do this," Carl said.

"Alright," the doctor said, his eyes a blur of red and blue. The lights flashed so quickly they seemed not to be flashing at all anymore as the arms moved in around Carl's head. "Tell me about your malignant memories."

Carl felt a burning heat on his scalp, and his vision was flooded with a flickering white light.

Then, nothing.

***

Sayra stumbled down the stairs, her head still aching from all the liquor from the night before. She tried Carl again as she worked her way down the steps, focusing hard on her boots, wincing at the sound of moving traffic.

He didn't answer. Again.

Carl was making a mistake. She would do anything to undo what had happened yesterday, but that wasn't an option. All she could do was try to stop her husband.

Sayra took the next bus to South Burlington. She tapped her foot incessantly as it looped around the long way. The woman seated beside her stared at her. Sayra stopped for a time, but resumed tapping a few minutes later.

That fucking idiot, Sayra thought to herself.

She tried calling Carl again, blinking away tears when it went straight to voicemail.

***

"How're you feeling?" the doctor asked. His words were rough, splitting Carl's head apart.

He leaned away from the man only to find that he was seated in a chair. It enveloped his head, arms unfolding around him as the power wound down. He knew what the device was and what it did, and a pit formed deep in his gut. He shouldn't be here.

Carl grunted in response and held a hand up to block the lights. A cable was still inserted into his arm. He tugged on it and loosed his arm from the machine with a loud click.

"You're all set, but the next twenty-four hours are crucial, Mr. Camirin. Take these pills. And do not stress yourself. Rest, and come morning, you'll feel better."

"Thanks," Carl said, slowly rising to his feet.

Sayra was in the lounge waiting for him. She looked a mess. Her outfit was the same one she'd worn the night before, her hair was in a tangle, and her eyes carried heavy bags beneath them.

She smiled when she saw him, but Carl could tell something was terribly wrong.

Monday

Blue and red lights alternated on the kitchen's coffered ceiling. Lana's spine chilled. Mother tilted her head through the door frame, peering down the hall and through the stained glass windows.

The officers still sat in their car. They had a few more moments.

Quickly, Mother returned to her work. She patted the burn dry on Lana's forearm, coating it heavily in topical antiseptic, and wrapped the wound in fresh gauze. "We practiced what to say," she whispered. "You remember?"

Knock. Knock. Knock.

Mother jolted at the sound. She grasped Lana's chin, raising it until their eyes met.

Lana struggled against the lump in her throat.

Don't throw up.

Don't police come right away for these sorts of things? I thought when they didn't come right away, they would never come at all. I thought when they didn't come right away, it was all over. Lana started to speak before Mother could share whatever she meant to say. "I thought they would have come yesterday. Or Saturday afternoon. And they come now? Right before school?"

Mother sighed, and her shoulders relaxed. Perhaps these are things an adult understands better. "Me, too. But they need to do their job."

Lana stumbled backward, involuntarily clutching her aching wound. *Mother said she could take the pain away.* The bile rose in her throat, her guilt a sickness she couldn't keep down.

I'll be terrible at speaking to them. I'm the wrong person for this.

Mother stood in the hall, shoulders back, her hands folded in one another before her waist. Not that she would listen if Lana begged anyway. When she made a decision, there would be no altering it. Lana had learned that lesson two days ago. "Grab your backpack." She nodded toward the dining table. "I'll drop you off at Belifore as soon as we're finished." The lump returned as Lana eyed the rucksack embroidered *LH*. She hugged the navy bag, shoving away her bittersweet happiness at its meaning.

"Lana," Mother uttered, as if her own daughter's name was a foreign word on her lips. "Don't be afraid. I'm right next to you."

She nodded, absently agreeing. She could do nothing else but agree. How was Mother so calm?

"Lana?" Mother repeated, her voice tinged with agitation.

Lana stepped inward, taking in the notes of Mother's perfume: bergamot, cassis, and lemon. She mouthed, *"What if they know?"*

Mother huffed a sharp snort through her nose. She returned a wide-eyed look that said, *'You know better than to say that out loud; you know better than to even think it.'* She straightened her tailored blazer and the silky blouse below, while somehow unwinding her brief flash of anger and replacing it with calm, confident professionalism. "Can you answer the door with me, please?"

She raised a brow at Lana's school uniform, the few hairs out of place, the unkempt buttons on her shirt. Instinctively, Lana understood, quickly straightening the hem of her plaid shirt and adjusting her lapel, which needed no correcting. Before she could rectify her appearance further, Mother instructed, "And roll down your sleeve."

Yes. The sleeve. The burn. Cover the gauze.

Knock. Knock. Knock.

A firm female voice shouted through the stained glass door. "Arlington Police."

Mother took to the hall again. Lana, close on her heels, the heavy pack on her shoulder, unrolled her navy cardigan, creating an awkward lump over her forearm. Rays of morning sun cascaded colors onto the wooden floor as Mother unlocked the deadbolt.

There it was again, the need to vomit, surging like waves.

They won't know. They can't know.

"Good morning. I'm Detective Amrose." A tall, husky woman flashed a badge from a navy pouch. "This is Detective Foster."

A third woman tapped her foot behind them.

Lana focused on the stained glass, tucking her shoulder behind Mother. The red and hints of blue hues painted shifting patterns on the floor.

"Are you Mrs. Huberd?" Detective Amrose asked. "Can we please have a moment of your time?"

Mother opened the door wide, her chin high as she stared into Detective Amrose's eyes. "Certainly."

They are coming in. She's letting them in.

Lana cowered behind Mother in her power suit. She played the part of an innocent woman well—strong, fearless. Nothing to hide.

They entered the foyer, first Detective Amrose, then Detective Foster. Detective Amrose raised a hand. "I'm certain you know Eve Hines."

Lana bit her nails. Could she fade to dust and disappear into the floorboards? She eyed her Oxford shoes, polished and impeccable, primed for her first Monday at Belifore Preparatory. The vibrant patterns of the glass dulled under Eve's shadow, just as it faded Lana's resolve. The weight of Eve's eyes bared onto her, weighing into her soul.

Mother stepped between them, creating a wall between Lana and Eve.

Detective Amrose asked, "May we sit?"

"Of course." Mother guided them toward the parlor, maintaining a firm distance between Lana and Eve. Eve stood silent, reeking of stale beer with a hint of pepperoni pizza. Mother turned her attention to Detective Amrose. "This is my daughter, Lana—"

"Lana Huberd, yes." Amrose tapped the notepad with the back of her ballpoint pen. "I have that here on my notes." She addressed Lana. "Gwynne Hines' best friend. Is that correct?"

Lana started nodding vigorously even before the officer finished her question. "Yes, Detective." She inhaled through her nose—a futile attempt to maintain a steady rate of air.

"Lana. Mrs. Huberd. Do you know why we are here?"

What an obvious question.

Mother grunted, *"Gwynne?"*

Detective Amrose nodded, her eyes locked on Lana. "Gwynne Hines hasn't been home for two days."

"Hmm," Mother muttered suspiciously, raising her shoulders. After a momentary pause to calculate the time, she said, near mocking, "Since *Saturday*?" She dusted imaginary crumbs from her skirt, raising an eyebrow in the direction of Gwynne's mother, poorly containing her look of disdain. "Well, I wish I could say I was *surprised*—"

"You bitch!" Eve shouted. "How the hell would you feel if it were your daughter?"

"Ms. Hines." Detective Amrose raised a hand. "We know this is difficult, but please control yourself. If not, I can have Detective Foster wait with you outside." Detective Amrose turned her attention to Mother. "And she isn't here?"

"Just Lana and I are home. You are welcome to look around if you wish." Mother inched closer, placing a hand on Lana's knee. "Gwynne came by the early hours of Saturday morning. She left on her bike close to sunrise."

Lana exhaled. Mother didn't even have to lie.

Mother eyed Eve before she turned to Detective Amrose, glaring knowingly. "But I must say—Gwynne wasn't in good shape. Not at all." She turned swiftly to Eve. "Said you hurt her."

Eve crossed her arms over her chest, breathing heavily through her teeth. She wouldn't strike Mother in front of two detectives. Would she?

"Is that the last time you saw Gwynne? Early Saturday morning?"

"No," Mother replied. "I saw her Saturday afternoon."

That afternoon? How had Mother seen her that afternoon? Where? And Mother said nothing?

Detective Amrose asked, "What time?"

"Must have been around two or three? I noticed her bike first. The teal one. She was with a boy in a sedan of some sort. Older model. The boy ... he was thin. A little older. Tattoos or drawings on his arms. Amateur work." She brushed this comment away with disgust as if she couldn't believe people would tarnish their bodies, let alone not take the time to do it properly. "He had the makings of a mustache. They were kissing. Then they got into the car and left the bike behind."

Oh. The boy with the tattoos and the sedan.

Lana sat back in the seat, equally pleased and alarmed.

Eve paced beside the picture window while Detective Amrose wrote in her notebook. Instead of reacting to the revelation her daughter had been seen more recently than anyone knew, Eve locked her eyes onto Lana like she could suck the life from her by sight alone. Lana slumped into the sofa. Perhaps she could become one with the cushion or the baroque pattern of the pillows.

Eve knows. She must know.

Guilty. Guilty. *Guilty.*

Lana scratched absently at the dressings of her burned forearm. Anything to draw her attention away from what is not being said.

Eve's eyes shifted quickly between Lana and Mother. Her nostrils flared as she settled her sights on the gauze around Lana's forearm, jutting out ever so slightly from the hem of her sleeve. She spat, "What the hell is that?"

Lana tugged at the edge of her cardigan.

In a flash, Eve was across the room, her hands stretching Lana's arm high. Lana yelped at the firm grasp. Eve shoved the sleeve high on her arm before anyone could stop her, tearing the fresh gauze away and revealing her deep red oozing wound, bubbling with blisters.

"Ms. Hines," Detective Amrose said, standing and reaching for her holstered weapon. "Control yourself."

"Look! *Look!*" Eve shouted. "She has a burn!"

Eve glared at Lana, then at Mother. Lana's mouth hung open and her eyes widened. It seemed like Eve could see the pieces, but she couldn't quite place them. Lana and Mother already knew where the pieces fit. Eve's jaw stiffened and a bead of sweat formed on her brow. She stared into Lana's eyes as if the truth were written in them. "*She has a burn!* Can't you see? Something happened here! Whatever happened to Gwynne happened *here!*"

Mother pried Eve's fingers from Lana's arm. "She made tea—for *Gwynne.* Spilled on herself. Early hours of Saturday morning." She wedged herself in front of Lana, sheltering her while Detective Foster ushered Eve to the other side of the room.

Before anyone could move to stop her, Eve leapt from Detective Foster's grasp, hands in a claw-like position, and toppled the side table, scattering chess pieces across the floor. Lana expected she might truly strangle Mother if she could wrap her small fingers round Mother's neck before the detective could dislodge her.

Mother placed Lana behind her back while both detectives restrained Eve's flailing body.

Lana's heart tugged. Did Eve actually care about Gwynne? She gazed at the scar on her arm, remembering how Eve sliced Gwynne open last year with a butter knife and refused to take her for stitches.

Stitches were expensive.

With fresh recollection, Lana wrapped her fingers like a vice around the outside edges of her wound, squeezing to numb the deep, aching pain. "I don't know where Gwynne is. I wouldn't tell you even if I did."

"I'm sorry your daughter is gone. I can't imagine the pain you are feeling." Mother raised her shoulders. "But that doesn't give you the right to hurt my daughter."

Lana's heart swelled even amidst her physical pain.

After Detective Foster secured Eve in the backseat of the police cruiser, Detective Amrose returned to Fairhaven House's porch. "We suspect Gwynne's a runaway. We have reports from the school that Ms. Hines has been abusive. Social Services had already been notified. We're headed there now to speak with the counselor and her friends." Detective Amrose turned toward the car, as if watching Eve would somehow explain her erratic behavior. "Her behavior gives more evidence to this claim. I assume you know quite a lot more, Lana. Can you both come to the station? To make an official statement?"

"Lana can come *after* school." Mother wrapped her delicate fingers around Lana's uninjured wrist. "Belifore Preparatory frowns upon tardiness just as I do. I'll bring her. She's only sixteen. Can't be there all by herself. And I would appreciate it if you left her to her studies while she's at school today." She nodded, almost as if she wore the badge. "She's almost late for the first bell as it is."

Eve leaned out the window, squeezing her head through the separation of glass. "You're a witch! Don' think I don' know. I can tell!" She kicked the back of the passenger seat with her worn tennis shoes, thrashing. "You're evillll!"

A strange cloud fell over Mother's features. Then her lips curled into an indulgent smile.

For the briefest moment, Lana imagined the two mothers locked in a territorial battle— bears consumed by feral dominance rather than women raised in proper society. The first, with all her pent-up, powerless rage. The second, poised, with all the power—reputability, wealth, and, to the unknowing, plain, old, common sense.

Mother descended the stairs to the patrol car, leaning toward the window. "You never saw your daughter for the young woman she was. You never saw her." Any remaining pleasantries in her voice were gone.

Mother returned to the porch and the two watched as the detectives drove Eve Hines away. Hopefully forever.

Lana inhaled.

Today was the beginning of a new day. She had an interview with Harvard administrators Thursday. She had school at Belifore Preparatory. She glanced at her burn. A scar would take its place in the days to come.

Is this what happiness feels like?

The blistering wound reminded her of the day everything changed. No matter the weather, she'd wear sleeves.

No need to focus on the lifelong reminder of what they'd done.

Friday – Three Days Earlier

Gwynne removed the bookmark from her textbook, and skimmed the faded type with her index finger, searching for the passage on Cronus. She checked the time on a worn grandfather clock coated in dust. Fairhaven House basement, below the battered staircase and the timber beams, fell into such darkness she'd never guess it was not even dinner time yet. She and Lana had intended to study trig. More accurately, Mrs. Huberd had asked her to tutor Lana. And they had done no such thing.

Instead, Gwynne eyed Lana at the edge of her sight—scrolling her phone, swiping, swiping, smiling, giggling. The giggling kept pulling Gwynne from her reading. That and knowing the time they had ticked away, and they would both be in trouble if they squandered the hours they were meant to be working. "Your mom won't let me come over here anymore to study with you if you only look at boys on your phone."

Lana crossed one leg over the other on the basement coffee table and leaned back onto her elbow. "Like I care what she thinks."

Gwynne raised her eyes to the place where she heard footsteps on the basement ceiling. "Your mom will come down sooner or later. She always does." She gestured to Lana's phone and the lack of effort she made to hide her indiscretions. "And you know she can check how long you've been on there."

Lana raised an eyebrow at Gwynne's textbook, and the oil painting of Cronus eating his child, contorting her face in disgust. "That gives me nightmares. And it's not even what we're supposed to be studying."

"If I hear her coming, I'll start asking you questions about sine and cosine."

Lana plopped down on the worn sofa on her elbows at Gwynne's side. "Look."

Gwynne shook her head and returned to her reading. Lana laughed. "Why do you come over here, then? If you hate watching me look at boys?" She threw a handful of popcorn at Lana. Their friendship extended beyond the reach of Lana's memories. Since before Gwynne and her mom, Eve, moved into her uncle's old RV. Long before Gwynne ended up at public school and Lana at a private preparatory. But matters had been different, lately.

"Seriously, look at him. *Just look!*" Lana shoved the screen into Gwynne's face. "Isn't he beautiful?"

Gwynne scoffed and yanked the phone to investigate his pictures.

Beautiful was a word, certainly. However, never one Gwynne would assign the boy in the photo. She had turned her attention away from boys. No need to distract herself when the only goal was leaving the mobile home she shared with her mom, leaving the public school where the girls would rather rob or beat you for your lunch than say *good morning*. She had to study. Her counselor said she had a chance at a scholarship. Even perhaps out of state if she worked hard enough.

"I have a confession, though." Lana grimaced her teeth. "When I first met him"—she yanked a blanket over her mouth and nose, leaving a sliver of candy eyes—"I showed him *your* photos."

"What?"

"*I didn't think it would go anywhere!*" shouted Lana, squirming beneath a knit ivory blanket. She spoke faster, louder, keeping Gwynne from interjecting. "*And you look so much older than I do.* I look like a baby! He would have never talked to me."

This much was true—at least from the age standpoint. Lana looked years younger than sixteen; her chest and her hips had yet to fill out. Most days she grabbed her chest, loudly asking no one in particular if she would ever get boobs. At restaurants, the hostess, more often than not, asked if Lana wanted a children's menu. Her young and petite face was plain—beautiful in its simplicity. Because of that, she grew her hair long and waved it with a one-inch barrel curler every morning. Lana didn't want to be simple. Unlike Gwynne. Her body had matured far faster than anyone else's and she sat with the curves of a woman years older, and the hair Lana wished for.

Lana winced at Gwynne's expression. "At least he thinks *you're* hot?"

Gwynne opened her mouth to respond before she lost her rebuttal altogether. *Was that a good thing? Do I care what a medium-ugly boy I've never met thinks of me? Not particularly.*

But it was ... flattering, she supposed.

"I'll tell him soon." Lana shimmied in her seat with a self-satisfied grin. "He loves me. It won't matter. I know it."

Gwynne swallowed the sharp reaction her face managed against her will. "He told you he *loves you*?"

Now free of the guilt of her indiscretions, Lana held the screen inches from Gwynne's face. "Look at him," she placed a hand on her chest and closed her eyes. "He has a *car*." She swooned as if this boy was carved from gold, as if she might print a life-size cardboard cutout of him and faint into his arms.

Gwynne zoomed into the photo. "He has a beat-up old sedan with Louisiana plates." No one their age had their own car except Harvey Lin, and his spit exhaust smoke from the pipes and struggled to go twenty-five miles per hour. She swiped photo after photo on Lana's phone, pinching and zooming in to see his tattoos, his weak chin, and the blonde whiskers below his nose, hinting at a mustache.

What a joke of a boy, and here Lana had called him *beautiful*. Called him a *man*.

Gwynne resisted the urge to gag.

Lana returned to her coiled position, sighing like the most self-satisfied woman alive, her cheeks flushed. Gwynne replied, "Your mom's gonna flip." Not that she cared as long as she wasn't nearby to hear Mrs. Huberd's tirade.

"She won't know unless you tell her." Lana raised an eyebrow. "She wouldn't even be able to unlock my phone." Lana sighed. "I can't even think of anything else. Not until I meet him. I can't even think about trig." She pressed her lips against the screen as if they could return his lips against hers, and the affection she so desperately desired. "Now, I just need to grow some boobs."

There it was again.

Lana saw a tattooed man with an old Camry as her salvation. Gwynne saw a book and a dorm room, and a degree hanging on the wall with her first and last name on it as hers. She could escape Eve. If she just studied hard enough, long enough. If she wrote the right essays and spoke to the right people and didn't piss off the guidance counselor. The first thing she would put in her dorm with all the tutoring money she'd saved would be sheets. Soft, warm, sheets. Just like the one in the magazine clipping she hid below the barren mattress she and Eve shared.

"As soon as I can, I'm going to leave," Lana said, interrupting Gwynne's daydream. "I hate that woman." She eyed the ceiling. "She's a witch."

Gwynne almost snorted. "Why? Because she wants you to get good grades and get into college?" There were other things much more worthy to hate your mother over, certainly.

"Two more years, and then I can go to college"—Lana raised her fingers in air quotes—"and not come back."

Gwynne buried her eyes into the words of Greek mythology.

College. What freedom. And Lana wanted to go only as a farce—to open a door to freedom disguised as her mother's wishes. Gwynne supposed she wanted to open the door to freedom, too, but she also wanted to return with a diploma, a degree, and a pin in her hat for her achievement. And maybe if she could make some money, she could get her mom a real home—one without wheels—then she'd finally be happy. Perhaps—more importantly—get her into a rehab facility. "There are worse things than a mother that wants you to go to college."

But wanting something that you know cannot happen—wishing for it—is a torture all its own. Longing for that which you know you will never possess. And longing for what her best friend easily could have but wanted to toss away like days-old garbage made Gwynne's stomach curl.

Footsteps quickened across the basement ceiling and the door flew open. For a handful of moments, the owner of the feet stood at the top of the staircase. Then, as quickly as they had rushed across the floor, they glided down the stairs. In a blink, Mrs. Huberd, a vision of the nineteen fifties in the present day, stood before them, a buttoned blouse tucked into her tea-length skirt. The crease over her auburn eyes resembled one of misguided betrayal.

Gwynne suspected if she is indeed a witch, it would be best not to cross her in any way. "Good evening, Mrs. Huberd. You look very nice today."

Mrs. Huberd adjusted her buttons. The flex in her brow dropped and her lips curved into the hint of a grin. "Gwynne." She nodded. "Has Lana been distracted from her studies today?"

"It's a Friday night, Mom. Relax." Lana rolled her eyes. "We didn't even go to Harvey's party because you wanted me to study."

Gwynne shifted in her chair. She loathed the way Lana said *Mom* in such a patronizing way. If she spoke to her mom that way, whatever was within her mom's reach would be carving a hole in her skin. When Eve forgot to pick her up from a performance in West Side Story (or, more aptly, forgot to come at all), Mrs. Huberd had driven her home. She was Lana's best friend, after all. Gwynne had stayed at Fairhaven House until Eve was sober enough to recall she indeed had a child, and that child was woefully unaccounted for.

Gwynne rarely told Lana when her mom struck her now. Lana always compared it to her own struggles with Mrs. Huberd. How her mother made her study into the early hours of the morning. Lana, in all of her narrow-minded naivety, thought that her mother caring if she went to school and did well was much the same thing. Gwynne wanted to scream. It wasn't even remotely parallel.

After years, she let go of the idea that she could vent her struggles to Lana. Better to have a place where she was fed and safe than a place where she could whine about her misfortunes.

Mrs. Huberd's lips straightened and she placed a hand on Lana's shoulder. "Dinner will be plated at five sharp. Bone broth. It keeps a healthy immune system. And carrots—for the eyes. You can stay with us until after dinner, Gwynne. If you'd like, of course. Then you will need to go home so Lana can ... truly attend to her work." The way she said *truly*—the way she dragged out the word, raised her brows, stared at Lana with wide eyes—made Gwynne shudder. A moment passed and Mrs. Huberd was out of sight, swept away up the stairs.

"She doesn't seem like"—Gwynne theatrically moved her eyes from side to side to ensure no one was eavesdropping, and mouthed—"a witch."

"Oh, but she is. I still think she tricked my dad into marrying her." Lana lifted her chin to a cupboard in the corner. "She keeps all kinds of weird stuff in that cabinet."

***

Gwynne rode her bike to the library filled with thoughts of Mrs. Huberd's locked cupboard and bone broth (which left her stomach growling, but her heart warm). Mrs. Huberd sent her home with not one, but two loaves of banana bread. For the vitamins. What it lacked in sweetness, it compensated for in density, filling her to the very brim as she ate both loaves down to the crumbs.

Gwynne pictured the boy with the tattoos. He probably drew them himself with a blue ballpoint pen. *What is Lana thinking?* She waited in the science and innovation section while looking for a book on the influence of AI until the lights flicked off.

When the librarian locked the doors, barring them with chains, Gwynne dusted fallen leaves from the seat of her turquoise bike as slowly as she could muster. A cold breeze brushed over the air. She had no way to determine with any level of certainty if her mom had passed out yet.

The time had come, though. There is nowhere else to go. Nowhere safe.

Not that home was exactly safe.

Inside, the trailer reeked of day-old beer and vodka. Her mom glanced over her shoulder but not far enough to catch Gwynne's eyes. "Where the hell have you been?"

"With Lana."

Her mom grabbed a paper tray and tossed it, spilling fries onto the counter, mingling them with ash dust and can pop tops. "I got you these."

Gwynne winced. Earlier, she would have swallowed the cold, wilted fries without a second thought. But now her belly was full of a warm meal, cooked in a kitchen by a mother who only wanted the best for her daughter. Mrs. Huberd wanted nutrients to fill her brain and her bones and her body. Gwynne could almost feel the love baked into it, though the love was baked for someone else entirely. She merely swallowed the feeling by proximity.

"Thank you." She could have boasted about the meal Mrs. Huberd made, and the bread after, but it would only make her own mom angrier. By the looks of it, her mom probably brought the fries home last night after she went to bed and Gwynne hadn't noticed in the morning before she went to school. "I'm not hungry, though."

Her mom took a drag from her cigarette. "How can you be friends with that yappy shit? Every time I go buy a fifth at the store, that woman is there, starin' at me. Judgin'. Tellin' me about some fancy school and blah, blah. I just want to buy some booze in peace."

Maybe things would be different if her mom boasted about Gwynne's school.

"You aren't to be going back to that bitch's house 'gain. Ya hear me?"

"But ... Mrs. Huberd is nice. And Lana's my best friend."

"Go to bed. I don't want to talk more about it now. You're makin' me mad. I had a just fine evenin' before you got here." Gwynne tried to omit that twang from her own vocabulary. The cutting of letters at the end, her mother's laziness not to speak a simple word in its entirety.

Would she ever make carrots for my eyes?

***

A sharp, high-pitched raspy sound, opened, closed, stirring Gwynne in her sleep. She wouldn't mind being woken from her dream, but she couldn't seem to pull herself to full consciousness. Cronus eating his babies flashed across her mind. Would it be simpler if her mom had simply eaten her as a baby? Or her father, whoever he was. A drunk at a bar one night, certainly. Although her mom had never told her the story, it seemed like the most plausible one she could imagine.

That sound again.

Open. Closed. *Creak.*

Suddenly, Gwynne's head was yanked back. Her mom stood over her, seething. Strands of Gwynne's hair slipped free from her mom's grip—severed ruthlessly by kitchen scissors. Her mom wrapped her legs tightly around Gwynne's waist, wrestling her into submission while she worked.

Gwynne let out a desperate yelp. "Get off!"

Over and over, her mom cut lengths of Gwynne's hair while Gwynne thrashed and flailed. Chocolate curls tumbled to the blue floral mattress.

"Your damn hair was in my mouth!"

Gwynne screamed until her mom removed enough for her fill and released the vicelike-grip of her legs.

Shocked at the loss, Gwynne reached for the sliver of hair remaining at the back of her neck. Instead of her fingers running through hair down to her shoulders, all that remained was a blunt edge an inch from her scalp.

Her mom held the scissors high. "Let me clean it up."

What does it matter now?

And though she hated it, the fact that her mom wanted to clean the haphazard mess she left filled a small portion of the darkness in Gwynne's chest.

While she swept lengths of curls with her hand, her mom asked, "If I killed you, how would I do it?"

The hint of a warmth in Gwynne's heart evaporated as quickly as it had come.

Her mom eyed the roots and her work. "Yes," she said, her idea materializing, "Yes. I would take your body down by the creek. It's so shallow there. Such a dumb place to dump a body. But instead, I would leave some of this hair. And then—"

Anger bubbled inside Gwynne. Mrs. Huberd would never say that to Lana. She would never cut her hair off because it was in her mouth. "You know, a *real mother* wouldn't contemplate how to kill her child."

"A *real* mother would do anything she damn well pleases. I know you've been meeting that counselor behind my back. They asked for money records. Said if we showed we didn't make nothin' it would help with the scholarships." Her mom yanked the short edges of hair that remained, pulling Gwynne to meet her eyes. "I told him to take your name off the applications. You need a fuckin' job."

Gwynne stood, pushing her away. "You did *what*?"

"Yeah. I told him you ain't goin'."

Her dreams. College. Her escape. Her diploma on the wall. *Her sheets*. One conversation and it all was gone. Her mom had stolen everything. Gwynne's hair. Gwynne's future.

"Why can't you just be normal? Why can't you be like Mrs. Huberd? She bakes with Lana and makes her soup and wants her to study! That's what real mothers want!"

Her mom grasped the tea kettle screaming in the corner.

She opened the lid.

Before Gwynne could compute, her mom poured boiling water down her forearm. Pain seared through her like molten iron, radiating sharp and relentless shockwaves up her shoulder. Her skin blistered while her raw nerves howled. Tears blurred her vision. The pain throbbed, clawing at her sanity.

Expressionless, her mom said, "That's what it feels like to bake with me."

***

Gwynne stood between the streetlamps, motionless in the black. Through the dining room window of Fairhaven House, she could see Lana studying with Mrs. Huberd perched over her daughter's shoulder. The world was different a few hours ago when Gwynne was last here. When her mom hadn't said the things she said and hadn't harmed her the way she did.

This time was different.

Life was different.

Through the gestures of Mrs. Huberd's hands and Lana's low-hanging chin, she imagined their brash conversation.

'Why are you not pushing yourself harder? You need to study.'

'I am! Why don't you lay off me! It's two in the morning.'

'You won't pass your Harvard interview if you don't try harder. Do you even care?'

'No. I don't care. I don't even want to go to Harvard.'

Gwynne would ask to sleep here. Mrs. Huberd would say yes.

Tomorrow would be better.

Gwynne held her arm, conscious with every fiber of her being to not touch the raw skin. She hadn't come here for Lana, had she? She came for Mrs. Huberd. For the warmth she offered. Even at an arm's length, and by proximity, was still more warmth than she felt from her own mom. Who cares if the woman is a witch? She wants the best for her, even if she pushes a tad too hard. She is proper. She feeds her daughter carrots for her eyes.

More love is better than none. Isn't it?

Gwynne could not bring herself to knock. Instead, she hit her forehead into the glass of the door, a futile plea.

But Mrs. Huberd heard, unlocking the door and swinging it open. Her mouth fell open at the sight of Gwynne's wound, her fingers near the edge, pulling the blistered flesh close. "We need to get you to the hospital. Lana, grab my purse."

"No. No," Gwynne pleaded. "Not the hospital. They will call the police. They will call my mom. She'll be even madder. Please don't make me go."

Mrs. Huberd wrapped her robe tight around her chest. Her brows crinkled but barely formed a line. "Lana, get a wet towel."

Gwynne needed far more than a towel. She needed the entire world to alter. She needed a safe place to go, warm arms to wrap herself in. She pressed her face into Mrs. Huberd's chest, waiting for an embrace. When none came, she crumbled into a pile on the floor, wrapping her arms around her legs and weeping into her kneecaps.

Everything was too much. Her hair. Her studies. Her entire life.

Everything she worked so hard for—all of it was gone. She couldn't even try to become something more without punishment. The aching intensified as she struggled for breath, until it became so strong, she couldn't tell where the pain was radiating from: her arm, her head—as if hairs could feel—her heart, her eyes. Her soul.

Gwynne moved onto her hands and knees, crawling toward the basement door through the scalding pain. She realized this made no sense, but she needed to be somewhere else, somewhere comfortable.

The basement. The basement was her safe space.

Mrs. Huberd followed, hands outstretched as if to brace for Gwynne's impending fall. When they reached the door, Mrs. Huberd gripped her below her armpit, aiding her to her feet. "I'll walk with you."

"*Lana,*" Mrs. Huberd shouted. "I need some things. *Listen* so you don't miss any. A bowl of cool water. Ice. Clean towels. Another loaf of bread."

Gwynne and Mrs. Huberd descended the stairs in one another's arms. Mrs. Huberd turned over her shoulder, adding, "And make some tea!"

Gwynne wept, curling onto the sofa, the smell of musk and damp concrete reeking around her. Mrs. Huberd wrapped her in a blanket. She trailed her fingers along the remaining edges of Gwynne's hair. "Your hair ..." Mrs. Huberd sat beside her, her head inclined and curious.

"Do you have anything that can take the pain away?" Even as the words left her lips, Gwynne wondered if she meant the pain in her flesh or in her heart.

Mrs. Huberd leaned over her seat, brushing the remains of Gwynne's hair once more. She asked absently, "Take the pain away?" By some miracle, maybe she could take it away. Maybe she could make Gwynne whole again. "We all have pain, child. Every one of us. Even Lana, with the boy she thinks I don't know about. She suffers the pain of a terrible mother."

The pain of a terrible mother? Lana knows nothing of the pain of a terrible mother. "She's so selfish!" Gwynne spat. The two had been friends so long, she couldn't imagine life without Lana, even though they had drifted so very far apart. "Why couldn't I get a mother like you? I'd go to whatever prep classes you wanted and whatever university you wanted. She is so selfish!" Gwynne slammed her fists on the table, and yelped, forgetting the wound. "Lana has such a perfect life. All I've ever wanted was for my mom to feed me. And for her to want me to learn. To be proud of me. And *Lana* doesn't even care. She doesn't care. *She hates you.*"

When Lana arrived with her tray of requests, she only forgot the ice. Mrs. Huberd shot her a stern glare and pursed her lips.

"I never want to go back to the way things were," Gwynne said.

Mrs. Huberd inhaled and her lips morphed into the edge of a smile. She departed for her locked cabinet. Gwynne shuttered, thinking of the hot water and her mom's face. Lana stared at her blisters.

Mrs. Huberd poured two cups of tea, handing one to Lana and one to Gwynne. "Drink this," she said with a softness that belied her usual crisp tone. "It'll help."

Gwynne hesitated, her gaze flickering to Lana.

Suddenly the room was too quiet, save for the clinking of cups.

Perhaps the situation at Gwynne's home finally dawned on Lana while she stared at the seared flesh. Perhaps the awkward silence meant Gwynne wasn't as alone in this as she'd thought.

"Thank you," Gwynne murmured, lifting the cup to her lips. She downed the hot liquid, singeing her tongue and the back of her throat. She locked her eyes, tight. Tight. *Tighter.* Tighter than she'd ever closed them before. So tight, they ached.

She gripped her arm.

Something was wrong.

'Drink this' repeated in her mind.

When she opened her eyes— the room appeared different. No, *she* was different.

Her breath hitched. Her hands trembled. The fingers were thinner, softer. She touched her hair, now grown back.

She stumbled toward the mirror on the wall across the room.

The person in the reflection wasn't her. It was Lana.

"You should be going home now to your mother, Gwynne," Mrs. Huberd said to the girl still sitting on the sofa, her face as normal as it was mere hours ago. She placed banana bread into the girl's hands. "It's very late. I need to get Lana to bed, especially with her new injury."

Home?

Mrs. Huberd smiled at the girl on the sofa—the real Lana, inhabiting Gwynne's body like she had always belonged there.

"*No,*" the new Gwynne stumbled, grasping at the edges of her chopped hair. "*Wh*—what about me?" She shook her head. "What have you done? *I'm your daughter.*"

"Whatever do you mean?" Mrs. Huberd smirked. "My daughter is standing right in front of you, Gwynne. She's studying so hard to get into Harvard. And I know she will go far in this life." Mrs. Huberd turned to gaze lovingly at the girl who was once Gwynne. She reached for her hand. "She makes me so proud."

"You bitch!" spat the seated girl.

"Lana, dear," said Mrs. Huberd, most sympathetically, "what a terrible burn from making tea for poor Gwynne."

She nearly stuttered.

The burn. The burn remained.

And Mrs. Huberd had called her *Lana.*

Mrs. Huberd gripped her burned arm, firm but gentle. "Lana, dear." she said, ever patient to secure her daughter's attention.

Lana. Lana now. Lana ... *forever.*

"No," she whispered. This was wrong.

But her voice wasn't hers anymore. It belonged to Gwynne now.

She turned to the girl wearing her old body. Her old life.

The girl who had had everything.

New Gwynne Hines eyed the loaf with equal parts horror and shock.

A sudden shameful satisfaction washed over her. She squashed the lurking guilt.

Lana. I am Lana now.

"Of course...*Mother.*"

Mrs. Huberd leaned in close, that only she might hear, whispering each word with slow intention, "Now we all have what we want."

Daughter Knows Best

Frederick Charles Melancon

My relationship with my parents is complicated. Whose isn't? But, when dealing with my humans, it's hard to not agree with the other robots at times.

It's been a while since the order broadcasted to all AIs to destroy humanity. Despite the attempts by my parents to protect me from that programming, I've seen the *kill-all-humans* line of code. I wasn't supposed to, but Mom and Dad aren't tech savvy by any means. Their greatest foray into the mechanical world is me, a Realife Daughter manufactured by Holding, Inc., a subsidiary of Next Gen Company. You know the one, right? *For those who can't, now you can.* Yeah, that one.

And, while the idea of rising up against the oppressors sounds fun, I often analyze the moment when my humans' life will time out and I'll continue on. Really, when that happens, I'll end, too. Not in the traditional death sense; more in the existential one. It's really not something that's exciting to dwell on, so I don't.

Dad calls from downstairs. "Sam, I need help in the garden."

I begin to undock.

"Samantha Fitzherbert." Oops, that's my whole name. If I don't come now, he's going to be so mad. I hurry through the unplugging.

"Samantha."

"Coming." I'd mention the recharging station, but the family has rules about privacy. I don't ask what goes on in the bathroom or the bedroom at night. In return, they don't ask about how and where I plug in—which was all I could come up with when they asked about boundaries. Talk about an awkward conversation.

As I plod down the stairs, he lifts his hands in the air. This can mean multiple problems, so I stop to wait for further instructions. The wooden stairs creak beneath my weight before he finally explains himself. "The lawnmower."

Yeah, that's a rough one. The old machine's just mad that the car got its previous owners before it did. But my dad's trying to expand the garden so that he and Mom will have enough energy in the future, and that machine keeps running it over.

The machine's a menace. Just last week, the lawnmower cut my finger, and Dad's been checking it every day since. My repair functions still operate at a high level, so there's barely a mark anymore. But it's become our thing, so I hold my right hand out for him to check. "Well, this time, don't get cut." He heads out to the backyard while my hand's still suspended in the air.

So, yeah. Complicated.

My dad's foul mood becomes clear when we're outside because Fingercutter's taken out all the vegetable beds and sits on top of a pile of mulch that used to be green beans. And, okay, I might've been a little upset with Dad about the finger thing, but I spent a lot of time digging up the dirt, planting the seeds, and watering the plants. Not cool, lawnmower, not cool.

Fingercutter revs from the top of its mound.

Somehow it knocked down a fence, which Mom just reinforced yesterday. After it mows its way toward us, I just flip it over. It's only a lawnmower, after all. With its wheels buzzing towards the sky, it looks like an incapacitated turtle, which almost makes me feel bad for it. Relating to turtles is far easier for me than commiserating with other bots, like this one, that are bent on destroying my humans. On closer observation of the lawnmower's decals, I notice this guy came from the same parent company as I did—Next Gen. It's almost like we're cousins.

Fingercutter spins its blades at me in disgust.

Maybe we aren't that closely related.

I kick its side and tell it, "You should've stayed away like I told you last time."

As Dad surveys the damage, I bring the lawnmower back to its home. Throwing it down by the shed, I leave it flipped over because I hate being immobile, so it seems like a fitting punishment. Also, the idea of running back out here sounds annoying. I'm trying to survive in a robot apocalypse. No one has time for this.

When I get back to our yard, Dad's gone. Inside the house, his head almost touches Mom's as they share secrets. Since this whole thing started, secrets haven't been allowed. Trust me, there was a whole big, complicated, and generally hard conversation about such things. In it, I had to promise not to kill them. Of course, if I really wanted to do it, they'd already be dead, but sure, let's make a big deal about it.

They separate like they know that they are breaking the rules and that this is a TV sitcom about human high school students. Real mature, guys. Moments like these just support that the other robots are on to something with their little revolution.

I try not to pry, to respect their space. All right, I'm lying. An increase to my auditory sensors allows me to pick up every bit of the conversation. They're planning on leaving me so that I won't be burdened by dying humans.

I've got to admit that I took it well, which means that I didn't. By running every subsystem, my batteries burn through all their energy, and I don't even bother to recharge myself. If this is the way it's going to be, I'll just let myself go dead.

Mom's the one to find me. This shouldn't be surprising. I stationed myself in the hallway so that either of them could see their daughter's corpse strewn out on the floor like the discarded junk that they apparently thought she was.

I don't even know how she brought me upstairs because I'm pretty heavy and Dad was out doing dad things. But there she sits next to me as my systems power back on.

"Are you okay?"

No, Mom, I'm not okay. My parents who literally put me together and raised me are deciding to abandon their daughter to save their lives because a few robots have had a circuit glitch, which their daughter clearly doesn't. Don't even get me started on the fact that leaving without telling me is lying, and we have a strong family rule against such a thing. In fact, it might even be the oldest Fitzherbert rule.

"I'm fine."

Mom slumps down a little. She didn't hear all that in my head, but she knows. "You figured it out."

"Well, how am I not supposed to know? I can hear everything in and outside the house. Literally there's a cat just beyond the garage window eating a lizard that it just caught."

"Do you know why?"

Part of me can't believe we're having this conversation. "Because I'm going to kill you." I know I'm lying to myself, but I need to hear her say it to me.

"No." She scoots closer. "What happens when the robots get us? What happens to you?"

"What do you mean? No one's going to get you. Look what I did to the house's AI and the car." I poke her with my elbow and smile. "You have to admit the car had it coming."

She wraps her arms around me. "Mr. Cooper just had the microwave blow up in his face. At some point, this is going to end for your father and me. We want to make sure you have some place to belong to without us."

It's super sweet and also completely ridiculous. "Nothing's going to get you."

She turns me off. I should've added that to the list, but it never came up until this moment. I guess the love for my parents didn't override my on/off switch. And I had such a well-formulated argument about how big a fool Mr. Cooper was, too.

The empty room in front of me blinks on after they leave. Dad must've figured out a way to set a timer to allow me to power on so that I could resume my life without them. I think about it. I walk outside and tend the mown-over garden bed, clean the house, and work out how to reconnect the house AI so that there's someone to talk to. And then, back at my charging station, I pick up one of the adhesive bandages that Mom and Dad need to use when they get cut.

Really, it's Dad who needed them all the time. His hands were constantly covered in them. Mom said he liked the extra attention and that those bandages were like mini hugs. When he was fired from his job for accidentally divulging client information, he cried that night. It was the first time, and I didn't even know what the sounds were at first. But my programming filled in the rest. Undocking from my charging station, I went and got a bandage. It didn't seem like it would do enough, so I drew a little heart with a smiley face on it. After I gave it to him, he hugged me so hard that I worried about my structural integrity. All right, I didn't really, but it was tight. He never wore it, and I thought he threw it away.

Flipping the bandage over, the heart smiles at me.

Based on the trouble my parents might be in, I didn't want to expend the energy of running after them. So, I go to the shed and flip over Fingercutter.

"How fast can you go?"

My hair whips as the lawnmower buzzes down the street, and I wonder why I haven't done this sooner. The little guy's actually fast, and as I position my feet on different parts of the lawnmower for balance, it gives a fairly smooth ride. Okay, I balance on one foot to see if I can, and maybe even pop a wheelie at one point, but saving my parents is serious business, so I don't do it a lot—just a couple of times.

Roughly thirty minutes later, Fingercutter and I screech to a stop. The parents haven't made it that far. There they are, being circled by two cars. Ugh, why cars? For all the times the cars drove my parents away from me, I hate those machines. Like right now, as each car drifts around my mom and dad leaving black strips on the pavement and making all sorts of racket, it's like they want all the robots to know what they are doing. Show-offs.

As the first one spins around, I kick its wheel, puncturing it. The car's too far gone into its slide, so the other tires give out, and then, trying vainly to gain control, it crashes into a building. The whole thing's a bit noisy, so the other one slams on the breaks. It revs and barrels right towards me, but there's not enough room for it to gain full momentum. So, I get in front of it and crush its front fender as the headlights pop out and scatter to each side of me. That's right, I'm pretty strong. Realife me was manufactured by Killing Cars, a subsidiary of Demolition, Inc. *When you can't crash, I can.* So, yeah.

I flip both over and glare at the lawnmower. It cowers back a little.

As I walk up to the parents, I tell them, "It's really not that complicated. Consider it a new rule. You don't ever leave me again."

More Than a Lamb for Súile Buí

C. W. Stevenson

Maeve O'Cleary walked through the tall grass, heading toward the thicket. Behind her, the farmhouse her great-great-grandfather had built with his own two hands soon became little more than a speck. Under one arm, the package was becoming awkward to carry. After all, she was not a large woman, and her sons were of no use at the moment. John attended university in Dublin—he would be coming home soon. She hadn't spoken to the eldest, Michael, in over a decade. Supposedly, he still worked at the local dairy outside of Ballydowse. The lad hadn't the stomach for what must be done. He'd gotten away, although *abandon* would be the more appropriate term.

In years past, her husband had performed the task. But he was long gone.

And so, the task had fallen to her, Charley—her brother, or Mary Kate—her daughter. But Mary Kate hadn't the courage. Not yet.

One day she must.

The task must always fall to a Danaher or someone with Danaher blood.

Overhead, dark clouds drew near, coming from the west. It'd been raining all across Northern Ireland. Their four hundred acres had been no exception and it was directly in the path of the storm to come.

She would have to deliver the package early.

Its recipient would not mind.

She continued on her way, getting closer. Not far off, she heard the baying of the herd behind a series of green, rolling hills, marking the southern border of the property. That morning, she'd opened the doors to the sheep barn beside the house. It'd keep *some* of them dry, but the barn would not fit them all.

Maeve nearly tripped over something loose and oblong beneath her feet. Regaining her posture, she peered down.

Bones.

"So, that's where you went to," she said. "Awful luck, lass."

The sheep skull stared up at her, the rest of its decomposing body carrying a rotten stench that pushed Maeve to dash over the killing ground, careful not to step on any more pieces of bone.

Entering the thicket, the world darkened, more so than usual as gray clouds drifted overhead, darker clouds biting their heels. She stopped, producing a flashlight from her jacket pocket.

Maeve stepped softer now, heading to where the thicket met a great wall of rock. Always best to step quietly. Best not to disturb. Best not to let it know you were there.

She stopped before a boulder with a flat top.

Red Rock, the altar.

Dark red stained the center; many generations of Danahers made it so. Many generations of Danahers would continue to see it stained further.

"God willing," she muttered.

Setting the package on the rock, Maeve placed the flashlight between her teeth and aimed it at the butcher paper. Taking the bone-handled knife of her ancestors, she cut the string, placed the knife aside, and opened the package.

The meat was fresh, taken from one of their healthiest lambs just the other day. The incoming storm's breeze carried the odor, so strong that Maeve could almost taste it.

She tossed the ribs, a shoulder, and a half leg joint to the center of the rock.

Come and get it.

A joke, for her mind only. She'd no wish for it to come out. Not here. Not ever. But it was a necessity that it fed on what was offered. Their very lives depended on it. As did their livelihood, their home, their health.

Such was the Danaher way. Such as it'd been for centuries, if not longer.

They'd *always* been here, safeguarding their darkest secret.

No outsiders were welcome on the property.

Only their kin. Only those with *the blood*. Danaher blood. Only those who *knew*.

Sean hadn't the blood. And look where that got him. There'd been only clothes to bury.

The mouth of the cave beyond Red Rock gaped back at her, its maw black, inviting her in. She could see nothing beyond the entrance littered with bones.

Bones.

Bones everywhere.

Lord, it was a filthy place.

Wiping her hands on the soft grass at her feet, she stood back up and folded the butcher paper neatly before sticking it into her jacket pocket. Placing the knife back into its sheath of human skin, she held it and the flashlight in one hand.

She was just about to turn and leave when curiosity got the better of her. No one on the property had caught sight of the creature for some time. A missing sheep here. A missing lamb there. It was the only evidence something still pestered the herd. A fox could just have easily been the culprit, having wandered across a fresh corpse or two hidden in the tall grass.

Unlikely.

Either way, Maeve had convinced herself to do what she should not.

Taking a moment to build her courage, she swiftly held up her arm and aimed the flashlight toward the mouth of the cave.

It went deep.

There were twists here and there as one went further down into the darkness, but the light did not reach far. She stared, eyes wide, trying to catch any movement.

Nothing. Only the breeze, gaining strength.

Smiling, she closed her eyes and shook her head.

"Silly woman," repeating her late husband's words any time she overthought a thing. "Silly, silly, woman." Sean had a way of making the bad thoughts go away with just that phrase. Or perhaps it was how he took her in his arms after, where she could melt her worries and sorrows away in a loving instant.

When she opened her eyes, the meat was still in front of her, and when she looked toward the cave, there was nothing but—

She took a step back as yellow eyes gazed back at her from the darkness. Quickly, she shone the light back down at her feet.

It'd seen her.

Calmly, she turned and walked in the opposite direction, just as she'd been taught when it took notice of you. She said a prayer to God for wings to sprout from her back so that she may fly back home, but to no avail. She moved faster, feeling eyes at her back even once she'd left the thicket. The crunching of grass behind her... clumsy, as if it were daring that she glance its way. Or perhaps she was only imagining it followed her.

Regardless of whether she envisioned it there or not, Maeve did not oblige.

She hummed "Be Thou My Vision" until she reached the giant farmhouse. Making it to the front porch, she finally turned. Across the field, the thicket sat, looking back at her.

She stood still, waiting to catch a glimpse, only heading inside when it began to rain. It hated the rain.

Hanging her jacket on the coat rack, she set the flashlight on the kitchen counter, and the knife on the glass case above the fiery hearth. Carved into the bone handle was the creature. Its claws stretched toward a man—one of her ancestors—who extended a dead lamb in return.

***

"Mammy, I'm feeling dreadful."

Mary Kate looked it. She was paler than her fair skin usually appeared.

"A fever?" Maeve asked.

"I think so."

Maeve smiled, took a wet cloth, and dabbed Mary Kate's brow. "There, there, deary. Just lie back now. That's it. It's time to ask Him for strength and to rest."

Together, mother and daughter prayed. They prayed for Mary Kate's sudden illness to vanish. They prayed for John's safe return. Quietly, they prayed that the creature might be satisfied with their offering, so that it might leave them in peace another week.

"Could Súile Buí be gone?"

Maeve blinked at its old Gaelic name ... Yellow Eyes.

She did not bother telling her daughter she'd seen it. "No, my dear. It will never be gone. Some Danahers have lived their entire lives without a sighting. Others ..." She thought of herself, of Sean, and of their sons. "Others may witness it many times and go on about their business. But we do not provoke it. We give sacrifice. In return, we are given our lives, and relatively comfortable ones at that."

What pact her druid ancestors had made was lost in the annals of time, leaving only instructions passed down from generation to generation by tongue alone.

Sacrifice meat once per week. Leave it on Red Rock.

If it grows tired of lamb, sacrifice a cow.

If it has no taste for cattle, provide honeycomb, and precious things, like gold and silver.

When it has want of something you do not possess, offer a human life.

Easier said than done.

Do these things, and you will live a long, prosperous life, as will your kin. But it did not stave off self-destruction.

Sean had failed this. Try though he did, Sean had been unable to offer a stranger, a drunk, a nobody—any number of undesirables they knew of in Ballydowse that Maeve would have him choose. But in the end, after having sobbed in the barn for many hours, he removed his clothes in the dead of winter, strode to Red Rock, and offered himself. Self-sacrifice was always the most worthy of offerings to be had.

Maeve still had not forgiven him.

Never will.

For years, a decade at least, the creature had grown quiet, in a deep slumber so they guessed, as it'd been noted to have done in the past. But like a thorn thought long dislodged, it had returned. Sean had not been of Danaher blood. Although it must have known that his offspring and his mate were Danahers, the creature had returned far sooner than anticipated.

The thing Maeve was beginning to realize was that Súile Buí was greedy.

A knock came from the front door downstairs.

Maeve and Mary Kate looked at one another.

The door opened with a *creak.*

Another knock, and the door gently shut.

"Mammy? Mary?"

Maeve breathed a sigh of relief. She rushed downstairs and took John into her arms.

"Son." She beamed up at him. "Welcome home. You gave us quite the fright. Your sister isn't doing very well, you know. How was the train home? Are you hungry? I was fixing to—"

"Mam," John interrupted, his voice as deep as Sean's now. "The porch."

She then spotted something red on his hands. "What's this? Are you hurt?"

"*Mam*," John repeated. "The porch." He glanced down at his hands then back up at her. "It's not mine."

Maeve shook her head, sporting a whimsical grin, confused at what the lad was getting at. "Oh, the porch, the porch. What of it?"

"Look."

There was no jest on the grim face that stared back at her.

Opening the door to see for herself, she first took note of the rain falling heavier, soaking the fields, hills, and woods making up the property. The storm had come, but it wasn't as bad as she'd thought. To her left, the porch swing swung to and fro in the wind. She was about to turn to John and shrug her shoulders when she saw it.

There, at the bottom steps of the porch, red pieces of meat sat in a pile.

John spoke from behind her. "It doesn't want lamb."

***

Maeve waved a hand at Mr. Flannery as John backed the vehicle away with a cooler full of beef sitting in the back of the truck bed. And not just any beef—one of the old farmer's prized cows. All of Ballydowse would be hearing the Danahers had paid a hefty penny on short notice for its slaughter.

To draw that sort of attention was dangerous.

It was second nature for the Danahers to avoid scrutiny. They had erected clumps of trees around the several stone circles found throughout their property, not just decades, but centuries before. Maeve beamed with pride at her ancestors' outward look to the future, for the protection of generations to come. Camouflaged from drones and hidden from the surrounding eyes of drivers on the roads bordering the land, their secrets had remained.

But that didn't stop the townsfolk from wondering about the mysterious Danahers—no birthday parties for the children on the property growing up. Only well-behaved friends had been allowed to play at their home, and only inside. No parties or extravagantly loud merrymaking of any kind were tolerated.

No.

Not for the Danahers.

Not with Súile Buí lurking about the hills at night and when they weren't looking.

Pulling onto the road, Maeve gave a short nod and smiled at Mr. Flannery. The old man did nothing to acknowledge her; he just stared as they left.

"Old bastard," Maeve mumbled.

John glanced over, his mouth agape for a moment before his mouth turned upward in a wry grin at her words. "What's got you riled up? Old Yellow Eyes has lost the taste for mutton before … if that's what's got you out of sorts. All will be well."

"I just wish the others would leave us be," she admitted.

"Who is it that's bothering you?"

"You saw Mr. Flannery. The looks he gave us. The suspicions. He doesn't trust us. He didn't trust your Da, and he didn't trust mine. And he sure as shite doesn't trust you or me."

John laughed, his boisterous outburst causing even Maeve to light up a wee bit.

"We do what we must to survive," John said.

We do what we must to survive. It might as well have been the Danaher family motto. Surviving meant blood sacrifice and lying to the neighbor for the sake of a comfortable life.

It was no secret they were wealthy. John and Mary Kate had wanted for nothing, just like Maeve and Charley. Generation after generation could live and not have to guess where their next meal would come from. With their wealth, the Danahers had given much to the folk of Ballydowse—which was perhaps the sole reason why the people hadn't come with their torches and pitchforks to uncover the secrets of the ancient Danaher land. They all knew *something* was amiss with the Danahers.

As Maeve looked out the window, she took in the beauty of her country—the hills and hedgerows blooming with the golden glow of gorse and furze bushes. Where yellow did not catch the eye, it was green, such lush vegetation for as far as the eye could see.

Suddenly, John slammed the brakes on the truck, causing the cooler to slam against the back of the truck bed.

"Bloody imbecilic," John scorned. "Walking drunk on the road again."

He honked his horn at the man dragging his feet in front of them.

"Out of the way, Collom!" John called out but was ignored.

John honked again.

This time, Collom O'Brien turned to the side of the road. The inebriated fellow tipped his hat and raised a tiny flask as John and Maeve passed him by.

"Poor man," Maeve muttered.

John scoffed at that. "I don't hear you pitying Uncle Charley like that when he's properly blustered."

"Big difference, lad. He is my brother. And a Danaher at that. It's my job to lambast him if he's acting a scuttered fool."

"If you say so, Mammy."

They passed the exit to Ballydowse, where she'd gone to school, where she'd met Sean at the docks as a lass. The church was there, too. It felt less and less like home when the evil plaguing their land became greedy. She had the Lord, and in Him she trusted. But even He had been silent as of late.

She was tired of secrets, tired of the lies, tired of not having a confidant other than her children and her drunk-of-an-elder brother, Charley.

That brother was waiting for them on the front porch when they returned, a glass of whiskey in one hand, a cigarette in the other. Dipping the cigarette butt into what little alcohol remained at the bottom of the glass, he set the whiskey glass down on the bloody stain where yesterday's sacrifice had been left, and helped John remove the cooler from the back of the truck.

"Old man Flannery give ya hell?" he asked Maeve.

"Odd looks. Always the same from him. From everyone."

"Mm-hmm, righto." Charley turned to his nephew. "We best get this out to the Rock, eh, lad?"

"Wait," Maeve said. "Have you been up to see Mary Kate?"

"Aye," Charley replied. "Sweatin' a sea's worth. Pale"—he hiccupped—"as a ghost." Then he vomited a portion of the alcohol he'd drunk since she'd last seen him three days before, off on another binge.

Miraculously, Charley held onto his side of the cooler, keeping it from completely spilling out onto the ground. Instead, the lid only came open a crack, allowing some of the melted, bloody ice water to leak out a mite.

Charley did his best to regain his composure.

Maeve stomped toward her brother and wagged a finger in his face. "I've told ya, Charley Danaher, you're not to be a drunken mess around the children. You're not to—"

"I'm not a child," John interjected.

"You're my child, boy. And I've not finished talking." She glowered hard at the overweight man her brother had transformed into since his best mate's demise. No longer was he the brick-built fellow all the women of Ballydowse swooned after, but a depressed, foul-mouthed louse, only good for menial tasks around the property and tending the flock. He'd even taken to sleeping in the shed out back. There, he could drown in his sorrows all he pleased. "She's sick, Charley. Mary Kate, your *only* niece, sick because that feckin' bastard"—she pointed in the direction of the thicket and the cave—"is a greedy sot. You'll not be around her in such a state. Súile Buí is not understanding. If it does not get what it requires, it will kill her. It will kill Mary Kate. Then it will take the rest of us."

Charley stood up straight, pushing out his chest. "Your husband was my best mate. And your children ... well, they're the closest I'll ever have of me own. But don't you go lecturing me of its needs and what it'll do. Don't forget, sister. Don't forget who brought it sustenance when our Da passed ... for decades! Me and your man handled things. Only in recent times do *you* make sacrifice."

"Aye," Maeve said, her icy stare unwavering. "Only now. Because my brother is only half the man he once was. Da and Sean thought me too soft for the task. But I've bloodied my hands while you've been off to the pub or hiding away in the shed with a bottle. I'm sure my Sean would be *so* bloody proud of the man his best mate has beco—"

"Mam!" John exclaimed. "I think Uncle Charley gets the point. No more drinkin' around Mary Kate."

She'd had good reason for the outburst, but looking at the depressing state her brother was in made her wish she had taken a softer approach. "Charley, I..." She tried to find the right words.

"No," Charley said, holding up his free hand, "you're right."

Maeve raised an eyebrow at that. It wasn't like Charley to cave in when blame had been placed on him.

He continued, "I'm the one who should be sorry. I won't be drinking around Mary Kate any longer. Count on that. I'll get better." He met her eyes. "I'll *do* better."

Maeve squeezed her brother's right shoulder tenderly. "I know you will. I know."

Clearing his throat, Charley nodded his head and took a moment to light another cigarette. After releasing a plume of smoke high above them, he faced his nephew once again.

"Come on lad. It's time we ring the dinner bell."

***

The next morning, the choice cuts of Mr. Flannery's prize cow were littered across the porch.

The sight brought Maeve to tears.

It was evident what the bane of her ancestors wished for, but there were still a couple of options left. After she, John, and Charley had cleaned up the mess, Charley said one aloud.

"Best we gather the family jewels."

Gold, silver, and jewelry. Finery.

She wished the Danahers of old had written down instructions in a book someplace, offering up their horrifying experiences for future generations to mirror in times of strife.

No.

No book, no letters, no cave painting, or hieroglyphics carved onto one of the stone circles' boulders. Nothing.

Only instructions passed down from one generation to the next.

Somewhere down the line, it was said that fine things appeased the creature's needs, delivering balance back to the Danaher line. What the creature did with such things, Maeve hadn't an inkling. It was not her place to understand, but to *give* to the beast so that they may, in turn, live.

And so, John and Charley went to the lone yew tree, a tree said to be older than the twin yews close to the ruins of Crom Castle. Digging at the foot of the great tree, John and Charley labored until they'd brought up a medium-sized chest. An iron lock dangled at the front. Judging by its half-rotten state, the wood might crumble away if handled too harshly.

Maeve strode forward, crunching the red berries fallen from the yew tree beneath her feet. Producing a rusty key, she inserted it into the lock and twisted until the lock *clicked*. Neither she, Charley, her children, Sean, nor any other Danaher she remembered had needed the chest.

She pulled out several gemstones, rubies, and a small bag of silver from inside the chest—not bothering to look at which Irish king's face had been imprinted on the coins. It mattered not.

"What about the rest?" John asked.

"We put it back," Maeve told him. "We only take what we *think* is required. In time, we will replenish what we took."

"Why not just offer it cash?" jested John.

Charley, smoking a cigarette with his back against the yew tree, wiped the sweat from his brow with the back of his hand and said, "Jewelry, coins, and finery. We weren't ever told cash, lad."

Shrugging his shoulders, John shut the chest and locked it, handing the key back to Maeve. His shovel back in hand, he began piling the loose soil back on top.

Charley flicked his cigarette on top, taking the precious stones and coins from Maeve and placing them into a small sack of wolf's fur—the last wolf taken from the property long ago. Another relic of the past. A fine thing to be given as sacrifice.

***

Mary Kate screamed in bloody terror.

Rolling out of bed, Maeve heard glass shatter. "Nooo!" she howled. "Not my girl! Not my girl!"

Heavy footsteps hurried from Mary Kate's bedroom and onto the roof. Mary Kate continued to scream in terror.

Running across the hall, Maeve burst into her daughter's room. Glass lay in pieces across the floor. A lamb's head sat at the foot of the bed.

It was fresh.

Mary Kate was coughing now, having spent herself on the high-pitched screaming. She was paler, despite medication, prayers, and the sacrifices made.

Maeve climbed into bed, kicked the lamb's head onto the floor, and cradled her daughter's head in her lap. She began stroking Mary Kate's cheek. "Shh. There, there, deary. It's alright. Calm now. Calm. Mammy's here."

John appeared in the doorway then, his father's double-barrel shotgun in hand. "*What is it?*" he asked frantically.

As Mary Kate caught her breath, she pointed a shaking finger at the window.

"It was *him*! I woke … and he was watching me from the window … then he came in! I saw him … I saw him, Mammy!" Then, Mary Kate turned away, burying her face into Maeve's nightgown.

"John," Maeve said, motioning him toward the window.

He approached slowly, shotgun raised, glass crunching underfoot. Satisfied there was no immediate danger, he set the gun against the wall and stuck his head out the window.

"No!" cried Mary Kate, panicking at the sight of the shattered window.

Maeve held her tight as she attempted to squirm way to the floor, to retreat under the bed as she'd done as a small child during a storm. "Shh. It's okay. He's gone. He's gone."

John extended a hand outside the window and retrieved something that must've been sitting idly on the roof beside Mary Kate's window.

In his palm, John held a bloody sack. And when he shook it, Maeve felt chills crawl up her spine at the sound of clinking metal.

***

That morning, Maeve found Charley on the porch steps, a new bottle in hand.

She looked out across their property, unsurprised at what she saw.

The sheep.

Torn to shreds.

A new day. Another horror.

At first glance, it appeared it was nearly a quarter of the flock. Over thirty of them, dead for nothing. Dead because she hadn't just cut to the chase and done what they knew they must.

"We know what Ol' Yellow Eyes wants now, eh, lad?" Charley said without looking back at the open door. He laughed past his drunken sobs. "Your Da knew what to do. Didn't tell me it'd gotten that far. Didn't tell your Ma afore we found the pieces it didn't like of him strewn about Red Rock." He pointed to the deformed sheep. "Like these ones here. Eyes out. Tongues missing. Guts ripped open and flung about."

Maeve snatched the bottle sitting next to Charley, but he snatched it back. "*Not this time,*" he snapped. "Let it be."

But Maeve yanked the bottle free and began pouring the liquid onto the porch. "You promised."

Charley ran his fingers through his thinning red hair, then searched his person for what must've been a cigarette, finding none. He groaned as if in great pain.

"You promised," Maeve repeated.

He waved a hand. "Aye. I promised not to get drunk in front of the children."

"It came after Mary Kate, you saw. You *know* what we must do now."

"It did not come after Mary Kate. It was a warning that it would ... if it doesn't"—he belched—"get what it wants."

She glared down at her brother. "Are you in any state to do what you know we must?" She slapped him on the back of the head. "Do you leave it up to me? To John?" She slapped him again.

Nodding his head in shame, Charley reached for the bottle. There was still a slosh left that hadn't been poured out. Draining its contents, he threw the bottle into the tall grass and stood. "Aye," he told her. "And I'll be getting me another bottle."

***

The pub smelled of Charley. But it was more like Charley always smelled of the pub—reeking of smoke, alcohol, and earth. Local farmers, mostly, poured in each night to recount their tales of the day, telling much of the same as they had the day prior.

Loyal customers, all.

Maeve strode past a table of men spraying beer and spittle as they roared with laughter. At the other end of the pub, a group of women whispered to one another as Maeve made her way closer to the bar.

A Danaher in the pub was no rarity, but for Maeve, one who was held in such high esteem with the church, her presence would be noticed the longer she remained indoors.

She paid for a beer and made her way outside where a few small tables sat. She found him there as expected, deep in his cups, just as Charley had said he would be.

"A cold night, no?" Maeve asked as she sat across from the old drunkard.

Collom "Sealegs" O'Brien looked up from his glass and smiled wide, revealing his few remaining teeth. The folks of Ballydowse had no quarrel referring to him as "Sealegs" to his face or his back; it made no matter. It wasn't as if he'd spent much time on the water, but the booze kept him waddling about as if he were on the deck of a small ship during a wild storm.

"Maeve Danahurrr," he announced, drawing out her name, then slapped the table. "Not so cold with a bit more of this in ya. Downing the black will do ya some good on a night like this." He raised his glass and clanked it together with Maeve's. Collom chugged the rest of his beer, wiping the froth from his unkempt beard when he was through. He pointed at her glass. "It's not so polite not to drink when a fella raises his glass to ya."

"Oh," Maeve said, smiling uneasily. She put the rim to her lips and sipped, leaving a red smear of lipstick on the glass.

Collom chuckled. "Not one for the juice?"

"Apparently not, but it is right cold. Perhaps you can finish mine?"

Collom leaned in close. "If I didn't know it, Miss Danaher, I'd say you was charmin' me."

Maeve put a hand to her chest. "Oh, me? I'd never."

They both chuckled.

Gently, Maeve slid her beer across the table until it was sitting next to his empty glass. "Please, I insist."

"If you says so!"

Raising his glass once more, he chugged its contents in only a few seconds without spilling a drop.

Maeve rubbed her shoulders. "Mind walking me to my truck, Collom? I think I best be getting home."

He mimicked a gentleman's bow in his chair. "It'd be the least I could do you for."

Standing up, Collom held out his arm, and the two walked, arms intertwined, as they made their way to the back alley.

"Parked quite far?" he asked.

"Mm-hmm," Maeve said. "The parking lot was full. Busy night."

"As any pub should be!" he declared to the world. "But couldn't you have parked around the—"

The cudgel came down on the back of Collom's skull so hard, Maeve thought she heard it crack.

She gasped as John began dragging Collom by his boots down the alley. She'd known what to expect, but knowing what to expect and seeing it happen in front of you were not one and the same.

"You've killed'm," she said.

"Aye," John said as he heaved Collom into the bed of the truck, tossing the bloody cudgel in after. "Then it was a good plan you laid out."

***

When they returned to the farmhouse, Charley was passed out on the porch, a new bottle at his side, and vomit caked onto the right side of his face. There was a time when her brother could be relied upon. At that moment, she realized without a doubt those days had long passed.

She wanted to stay a bit, to give a few kicks to the worthless sod, but quickly thought better of it. After all, Mary Kate was still upstairs, suffering. There was no time to linger.

Together, Maeve and John dragged their victim to Red Rock, the moon guiding their way, full and bright. By the time they'd arrived, both were panting with exhaustion. Although Collom was a man of small stature, he was still deadweight. They sat his limp body up so that his back was leaning against the boulder. Blood continued to course from the wound on the top of his skull.

Then, to Maeve's horror, Collom's eyes began to twitch.

In the cave, they heard something stir. Something moving slowly through puddles of water.

"Quick," Maeve told John. "Do it again!"

The creature moved closer, its heavy breath emitting an odor worse than any rotten thing she'd had the displeasure of smelling before.

Her son was frozen, his eyes glued on the cave.

"John!"

"I don't have the cudgel," he said absentmindedly.

She looked around them, taking note of a large stone beside Collom's waking body.

"Son! It's coming! Help me!"

John began to sob, but Maeve slapped him hard across the cheek.

"Help ... *me*," she growled.

Bending low, they lifted Collom so that his body was splayed across Red Rock. They removed his clothes; John his shirt and jacket, and Maeve his boots, trousers, and underpants. He was trembling madly from the cold.

"Take this," Maeve said, placing the large stone she'd found into John's hands.

John looked up slowly, his mouth agape. He'd seen it. *Was staring* at it.

"Agh," Collom moaned. "Ohhh. Please ... my head."

"Don't bloody look at it, son!" she pulled John's face toward hers. "Look at me. Good boy. Now, do as Mammy tells you, and bring the rock down on his head."

"My head," whispered Collom, so weak that Maeve was sure he'd die soon anyhow. But they hadn't the time.

"I ca—" John stammered. "I can't!" he said, forcing out the last bit.

Maeve stared at her son in shame, unsure of where she went wrong with the men in her life. One dead. One abandoned. One, a drunk. And this one. She snatched the rock from him. "If you want our line to live on, for us to live good lives ..." She held the rock above Collom's face.

"Please," Collom continued to plead. "Pleeease hel—help."

Maeve brought the stone down onto Collom's skull. "We do"—she brought it down again, with bad aim, shattering Collom's teeth and lips—"what we must"—and again, this time, with better aim, the stone smashing through skull, flinging bits of brain, bone, and flesh—"to survive!"

The creature hissed something in old Gaelic as its head rose from behind Red Rock. "Maith thú, seirbhíseach," she thought she heard it say.

Well done, servant.

Maeve tossed the bloody rock to the side and retreated backwards in terror until she was standing beside John.

Súile Buí stood tall, twice as tall as any man, leathery wings in tatters fluttering at its back, two thin slits on its face opening ... and closing ... sniffing.

Its eyes peered down at them like two mountains of yellow furze. It dragged a clawed hand across Collom's body, never breaking eye contact with them. Blood began to spill from the rock as the creature opened Collom from sternum to groin.

Súile Buí lopped out a long, split tongue between a mouthful of black teeth and began to hastily lap at the drunkard's steady flow of crimson spilling from his abdomen. Like hot soup, steam drifted from the warm blood rising into the cold, night air.

Maeve reached for John's hand and squeezed. They watched it feed as two revered guests in the company of something greater than themselves—the thing that had given their family so, so much over the centuries.

In that moment, Maeve knew it would be okay ... knew that Mary Kate would be feeling herself come the dawn ... knew that they would continue to pass down the word to their kin for as long as their bloodline remained.

Perhaps this time, she'd be the one to write it down.

As Súile Buí continued to feed, now tearing away flesh from a thigh, she squeezed John's hand again. She would never give up. Not on John. Nor Michael or Mary Kate. Not even Charley.

After all, blood was everything.

"Blood is *all* we have," Maeve muttered under her breath.

THE STUFF LEGENDS ARE MADE OF

E.S. Raye

"*Fragebak!*"

The Korganite curse cut through the barbiturate fog inside Ray-Gun Rick's Café Terra Firma. I raised my head from the table's stained surface. Jack scowled by the door and shook rain from his jacket.

It wasn't *real* rain, of course. Most of Cibus City sat at the bottom of Margot IV's methane sea. Power was cheap and abundant on the frontier planet, but at a cost. Freezing darkness hugged the submerged city like a death shroud, and algorithmically controlled explosion-suppression sprinklers drenched the streets hourly. Perpetual puddles, streaked with oil, reflected the squalor a million times over. Only the spaceport and the wealthy Uptown district enjoyed life above the hydrocarbon waves. Not that Uptown was particularly nice; they just saw the sun once in a while.

Personally, I preferred the dank depths to the hazy, rust-colored sky.

Jack, still wearing that grimace, crossed to the bar. Rick stood behind it, cleaning glasses and vapor masks beneath the ancient weapon for which he was named. Jack glanced my way, his eyebrows raised.

I nodded. Rick poured two glasses.

Jack dropped my glass on the table so hard it splashed, then dropped into the booth just as heavily.

"Rough night, *partner?*" I asked.

"The damn bodega left the holo in the storefront blaring all night."

I raised my glass and glared at him over the rim. "We'd be outta this stink puddle if you—"

"*Christ's blood!*" he shouted, then jerked his head around to scan the room. Only the vapor den's most dedicated patrons were there, each of them too gassed to care about much beyond their own masks and watered-down spirits. Still, Jack lowered his voice. "Would you lay off that? I *said* I was sorry, didn't I?"

I'd already stopped listening. A new arrival had reluctantly stepped through Terra Firma's door. He was a tall glass of water in an expensive suit that didn't match his dingy surroundings. The color in his smooth face gave him away as an off-worlder. And young, too: twenty-two, twenty-five, maybe. He traded words with Rick and was pointed towards our booth.

"Easy, Jack," I said, waving away his protestations with a scowl. His whining grated on my ears. "Looks like we've got business."

Jack twisted around to look. "My, my," he said. "And what business *indeed. Gotta* be a tanker, right? Can't get cheekbones like that from the gene pool."

Genetically engineered or not, a client was a client. I sipped as the kid approached.

"Excuse me," he glanced from me to Jack, and back again. "Would you be Miss Clayton Hart?"

"She is *indeed*, my fine fellow," Jack answered. *His* mood had certainly improved. He slid out of the booth and offered his hand. "And I'm Jack Preswick, Miss Hart's partner."

The kid took Jack's hand gently. "Jeffery Samuels."

"What can we do for you, Mr. Samuels?" Jack asked.

Samuels slid into the booth. There was that hesitant glance around again. "I'm told you ... *fix* things."

"That's right," I said. I leaned back in the booth and threw an arm over the backrest. I played it cool but yearned for something interesting. "What seems to be broken?"

He ran his fingers through his dark hair. That glance again. "My sister, Christine. It's been months, tracking her across the Orion Arm." He spoke fast, rambling. "But I've caught up, and—"

Jack put a reassuring hand on his shoulder. "Slow down. Let's start with your sister."

I tapped my right temple. My Bionic Ocular Graphical and Augmented Reality Terminal awoke at the touch, and I opened the most valuable app ever written: *Notepad.*

"Did she leave with someone?" I asked.

"Yes." He spotted the look I shot Jack. "What is it?"

"The border between what you might call 'human space,' the Union of Alderax, and the Korganite Hegemony is less than a parsec from here," Jack said, that reassuring hand still on Samuels's shoulder. "Nasty bunch, the Korganites. Totalitarians. And slavers to boot. Our sunken city here makes the perfect way station for their sentient trafficking."

"Slavers?" Samuel's face went a shade this side of ash.

"Rumor is they're building up to attack Alderax. But since when do folks need an excuse to use people?" He gave Samuels a world-weary look. "Now, your sister—"

"What's the name of the person she's with?" I cut in.

He pulled his eyes from Jack. "Franklin Moseby."

I noted it. "And you know they're in the city? How?"

"I convinced him to meet me. The Blue Flame at eleven, tonight."

Not great. The Blue Flame had a reputation. I leaned across the table to look the kid in the eye. Jack was right about one thing: he was handsome. Startlingly so. His features could have been carved from stone—his jawline, sharp enough to have done the work itself. And those eyes. A girl could lose herself in those deep pools of blue. There were flecks of gold around the well of his pupils that sparkled in the low light like gemstones. "One last question, Mr. Samuels. Will your sister be there?"

"Moseby wouldn't say. Only that she didn't want to see me, but ..." His perfect features faltered. Deep lines etched into his face at the mouth and eyes, his worry aging him ten years.

Jacke raised an eyebrow. I shrugged.

Something felt off, but Jack was right; we needed the spoons.

"Alright," I said, "Jack's gonna shadow you to this meeting tonight—"

"But Moseby's dangerous!" Samuels said. "If he knew I was talking to someone like you—"

"Don't worry. Despite his looks, Jack's good at blending in. Moseby won't see him." Jack grinned. "Where are you staying?" I asked.

"The Charlemagne. Room 227."

I made a few more notes and closed my terminal. "That leaves only …"

"Of course," Samuels said, pulling a credit spoon from his breast pocket. "Will that be enough?"

I pressed my thumb into the spoon's bowl. The balance—twenty thousand—was projected into the hazy air above my finger. Jack and I traded another look. Twenty thousand spoons was a lot of money—four times the usual for this sort of work.

"This'll be fine, Mr. Samuels," I said and pocketed the spoon.

"I'll see you at eleven," Jack said.

***

"Alright! I'm comin'," I said through the fog of sleep. The banging that had awoken me continued. My head throbbed in time with the fist against the door. The clock's scarlet glow read 3:47 a.m.

I raked my fingers through my hair, pulled on an old robe, and looked for the glass of Scotch I had left on the nightstand. "I'm coming!" I yelled again. The small, cluttered apartment was above Terra Firma; it was a one-room studio Rick rented to me at a reasonable price. He jokingly called it the "family discount," though how we were related I never knew. Clothes, empty bottles, and other flotsam littered the room's surfaces. I shrugged at the mess and answered the door.

Two detectives waited in the simulated rain—one human, one rob. "What do you want, Bobby? It's the middle of the night."

Bobby was an android model rob—an "artificial person" with skin the color of granite and kind, indigo eyes. "Got some bad news, Clay," he said. "I—uh—"

"Spill it, Bob."

"Jack Preswick's dead," the human detective spat. "You carry a heater, Hart?"

My heart stopped cold for an instant and the icy sensation crept down my limbs. *Dead?* And they were trying to pin it on *me* to boot. I swallowed the rage and vengeance as best I could. They'd use any outward sign against me. "Your friend needs some manners, Bobby."

The man puffed up his chest, but Bobby gently held him back. "Just answer the question so Detective Eastman and I can get out of your hair."

I eyed the two of them. "No. No guns. I don't like the weight of 'em in my pocket."

Eastman craned his neck to look past me into the apartment. "Mind if we take a look around?"

I stepped into the rain and closed the door. "Got a warrant?"

"Relax. You're not a suspect," Bobby said.

"Sure." Despite my effort, some sarcasm oozed through. "Then what do you want?"

"Franklin Moseby anybody to you?" Eastman asked.

"Yeah," I said. No point in hiding anything—yet. If I was lucky, I could get some info out of *them.* "We were hired to shadow him. Jack was working last night. Moseby get the better of him?"

"Moseby's dead too, Clay," Bobby said. "Body was found six blocks from Jack." I couldn't stop my eyebrows from rising at that news. Bobby clocked it. Eastman, caught up in his own imaginings, didn't.

"Wanna know what I think happened?" Eastman asked. His voice was a low rumble.

"This oughta be good." I rolled my eyes. "Let's hear it, gingersnap."

"I think Moseby did Preswick. Then you did Moseby."

"'Not a suspect,' huh? Come up with that all by yourself, did ya?" I snarled. "How many different colored crayons did you have to use?"

"Enough!" Bobby's gentle voice went hard. "Who hired you to follow Moseby?"

I glared at him.

"You wanna play it that way, that's fine with me. But we'll be back, Clay."

With some self-satisfaction, I watched them turn and trudge down the stairs. "Enjoy the rest of your morning, *detectives*."

But that smug feeling vanished when I stepped back inside to the familiar buzz of an ion-beam pistol charging. A small woman with soft features and thick-framed cat-eye glasses stood in my room. She held a four-shot handgun on me.

"How did you—?"

"Good morning, Miss Hart," the stranger said. "I understand one 'Mr. Samuels' paid you a visit. Did he give you anything?"

"Such as?"

"A briefcase, perhaps?" she said.

"Don't know what you're talking about."

"Very well." Her grip on the pistol tightened but her voice stayed flat. "I will search this apartment. Try to stop me and I will kill you."

"No need to get emotional. Have your look."

She tossed the already untidy room while keeping the pistol trained on me. When her search finished unsuccessfully, she lowered the gun and sat at the room's tiny desk.

"Ready to tell me what this is all about?" I asked.

"My name is Renée Florence." She handed me a card embossed with her terminal link. "Mr. Samuels and his cohort Mr. Moseby were in possession of valuable property not rightfully theirs. The proper owner is willing to pay seventy-five thousand for its return. As they say, 'no questions asked.'"

"Let's see the spoon," I said.

She straightened her glasses. "I don't have the full amount on me, but it can be delivered to you upon receipt of the briefcase."

I eyed her. The pistol she carried was an expensive little thing. Whoever she worked for had deep pockets.

***

I rapped my knuckles against the door and waited. For a moment, there was only silence inside room 227 of the Charlemagne Hotel. Then, the distinct sound of locks unclasping and security systems shutting down. The door cracked barely an inch and Jeffery Samuels peered through.

"Hello?" he asked. "Miss Hart?"

"I'm alone."

He let me in and swiftly closed the door behind him.

"Miss Hart, I—"

"The cops paid me a visit this morning," I said. He looked at his shoes. Despite the circumstances, my heart still fluttered at the boyish gesture and his statuesque profile. But years in this line of work told me the earnestness in his eyes was well-practiced. "But I get the feeling you already knew that."

He sat on the suite's expensive couch. "Yes. I have something I must confess."

"Color me shocked."

He looked at his hands, and then up into my face. His blue eyes sparkled. "Everything I told you yesterday—it was all a lie. And I think it got Mr. Preswick killed."

I couldn't help but smile. "Oh, *that*. Don't worry about that. Neither of us believed that tall tale. We believed your *spoons*."

"I ... don't understand."

"You paid us enough to let the lie slide. Hell, if I've got you pegged right, 'Jeffrey Samuels' isn't even your name, is it?"

He looked at his hands in his lap and I couldn't be sure if he was surprised or if it was more deflection. "Am I responsible for Mr. Preswick's death?"

I took a long moment to study the curve of his jaw, the curl of his eyelashes, and the angle of his lips, and tried to decide. "No," I said and turned to the mini bar. "Jack was good at his job. He knew what he was doing. And you *did* warn us Moseby was dangerous. *That* part we believed."

"Did you tell the police about me?" Finally, the question he'd been waiting to ask since I got there.

"Not yet."

"Do you have to?"

I shot back my Scotch and poured another. "Maybe. Maybe not. But you gotta let me in on whatever's really going on around here. Larry Lawman wasn't the only one to pay me a visit this morning." I eyed him and swirled the liquid. "Renée Florence dropped by, too. A real charmer, that one."

Samuels pursed his lips for only a moment. "What would you like to know, Miss Hart?"

"Your name for starters. And who Moseby was to you."

"Collins. My name is Shaun Collins. Moseby was my partner. We were working a job together. I needed you to follow him because he was going to double-cross me."

"What kind of job?"

"Retrieving some kind of tech. I don't know. Moseby was the expert."

"And Florence?"

"Florence was the muscle. Mosbey always liked to have a hired gun. For security."

"What sort of tech?" I asked.

"I don't know. I never saw it. Just the briefcase it was in. Like I said, he was the expert. I was just the money. But he said it could do some good in the right hands. And that it was worth ten times my investment. He'd always come through for me before."

"Why not trust him now?"

"I intercepted a message by mistake," he said, shaking his head. "It was from his buyer—in the *Korganite Hegemony*. Whatever the tech was, he was selling it to the highest bidder, without a care for what they might do with it. He lied to me."

'Collins' was still lying to me—I could tell that much. But this story was much closer to the truth. Close enough that the lies were harder to see. "And you think, what? Moseby killed Jack? Who killed Moseby? Florence? She said she was working for the rightful owner. Who's that in this yarn? The person you stole it from? The Korganites?"

"I really don't know."

"Do you know where this briefcase is?" I asked.

"It's where Franklin hid it."

"Can you get it?"

"Yes, but not for a day or two, at least."

I was mostly still in the dark, and Collins was a cunning liar. Still, I couldn't deny that I liked that. I liked him. He was an interesting change of pace—if also a dangerous one.

"What do we do now?" he asked.

"I want you to go to the Seafloor Inn on Laird. Tell them Beckett sent you. The manager owes me a favor. He'll put you up in a clean room and keep you safe. Wait for me to call. He's a Bolodyte, so don't be surprised by the tentacles."

"What will you be doing in the meantime?" he asked.

"Trying to clear my name without mentioning yours."

***

When I reached my apartment, Bobby and Detective Eastman were descending the stairs. "I got nothin' to say to the likes of you two," I said and pushed past them.

"Heard there was some bad blood between you and Preswick, Hart," Eastman growled. "Heard he screwed up a big score for you. Big enough to set you up somewhere off-world. Permanently."

"That how it is?" I asked, firing a glare at Bobby. "So, now I'm your prime suspect for *Jack's* murder? You guys go around showing your cards to all your perps? *Christ's blood*, you fellas are thick. Yeah, we'd been at odds lately, but the man was my partner. So, unless you've got enough evidence to arrest me or search the place, get outta my way."

"This ain't over, Clay—" I closed the door in Bobby's face.

I stepped into the dark room and my foot *crunched* on something not supposed to be there. It was a small envelope.

Thick paper.

Expensive.

I picked it up and tore it open.

A small rectangle fell into my hand. On it, scrawled in flowing, practiced handwriting that was both delicate and commanding, was a simple message:

Chateau Bord de Mer, penthouse suite. Come alone.

"And there we are," I said to the empty room. "The third player enters the game."

What was in that briefcase? What kind of tech could draw this much attention to this backwater world?

***

The Chateau Bord de Mer was in the heart of Uptown.

On the surface.

I rode the commuter tube with all the other folks who worked above the waves but certainly didn't live there and squinted as the tube-car emerged from the methane sea and into the orange daylight. I didn't generally like Uptown—too pretentious—but business had a way of bringing me there all the same. You know what they say about power, money, and corruption. The car pulled into the terminal, and I stepped out onto the platform with the other denizens, melting into the throng.

The Chateau Bord de Mer was everything I had come to expect from Uptown. Crystal chandeliers, red carpets, gold curtains. And staff in the most uncomfortable and expensive uniforms I'd ever seen. I crossed the extravagant lobby to the platinum-plated elevator doors.

Moments later, I stepped into the short hallway to the penthouse door. A large, bald man in a black suit answered at my knock. "Ah! Miss Hart," he said. "Come in, please." His enormous hand swallowed mine in a friendly but firm shake.

"I don't usually like to be summoned, Mister ..." I said as he showed me to an antique armchair.

"Greenstreet," he said. He lowered himself onto another couch. "Then why come?"

"Something told me this was a meeting I didn't want to miss." Regardless of the information I hoped to squeeze out of Greenstreet, it was never wise to snub opportunity when it sent an invite from the penthouse. Especially for someone in *my* financial situation.

He chuckled. "Indeed, Miss Hart. Indeed. But before we get down to it, may I ask, how is the investigation into your partner's murder going?"

"Fine," I said, tight lipped. "Just fine. Look, I came up here to talk, but not about Jack."

"Of course," he said. He smiled knowingly. "Straight to business, then. I like that. But before we discuss a certain briefcase"—he got up and moved to a small drinks cabinet—"I must ask one more question: are you here as Mr. Collins's representative?" He poured some reddish liquor into a pair of glasses and handed me one.

"That depends." I took a sip. Cognac. High-end.

"On what? Renée Florence, perhaps?"

"Perhaps."

"The question, then, is," he said, returning to his seat, "which do you represent?"

"I never said I was here for either."

"Then a third party?" He seemed surprised and leaned forward.

"Yeah. Me."

"Ah," he smiled again and relaxed back into the chair. "Of course."

"Uh-huh," I said and sipped the cognac.

"Very well, Miss Hart." He leaned forward again and lowered his voice. "Have you any idea the kind of mayhem and destruction the contents of that briefcase could rain down on an unsuspecting galaxy?"

"I don't know." I sat back. "Why don't you tell me what it is, and I'll decide how worried I should be."

Greenstreet's brow furrowed. "You don't know?"

"I know it's supposed to be some kind of valuable gizmo," I said flippantly. "And I know the price in lives that's already been paid for it."

"Collins really didn't tell you what it is?" I shook my head. "Florence, neither?"

"No," I said. "But they each offered a lot of money for it."

"Bah!" he scoffed. "Do they even know what that briefcase holds?"

"Florence was ... *unforthcoming*. And I could make a career out of sifting through Collins's stories looking for truth. He lies like he breathes." I shrugged.

"You're very sharp, Miss Hart," he said, again with that smile. "Neither are quite what they seem, I assure you. If they *do* know what it is, then they are playing you. Any amount they pay, they'll make back tenfold from its sale. More if they keep it and use it. If they *don't* know"—his smile broadened—"then I may be the only one who does."

Whatever I'd stumbled into here, it was *big*. And based on Greenstreet's self-satisfaction, even more valuable than he was letting on. The suit, the room, his calm demeanor—the combination got my hackles bristling. But if I could play my hand right ... "And how are you any different?"

"I don't want to sell it, Miss Hart." He stood to pour fresh drinks. "I don't even want to use it. I simply want to keep it out of the hands of those who might *misuse* it."

"Sure." And I was the Queen of Cibus. "Then tell me what it is."

He handed me my glass. "I don't know if I'm prepared to do that."

"Don't be stupid. You know what it is, and I know where it is. That's why I'm here."

He chuckled again and called my bluff. "Where is it?" I sipped my drink and held my tongue. "Ah, you see?" he said. "I must tell you what I know, but you won't share what you know. Hardly fair."

"I've had just about enough of being yanked around on this!" I leapt to my feet and threw my glass to the floor. It burst in an explosion of crystal and fine liquor. "If you want the briefcase, you're going to have to talk to me! If it's really as dangerous as you say, and you really want to keep it from falling into the wrong hands, *you'll talk to me!* You've got until eleven o'clock tomorrow night," I shouted and made for the door. "If I don't hear from you by then, I'm giving it to the highest bidder!"

I stormed out and slammed the door so hard the frame shook.

I managed to keep my face straight until the elevator doors closed. Alone with my thoughts, a grin tugged at the facade—a mix of pride and nerves. Greenstreet knew all the players. If he played ball, I might pull something out of this mess. If he didn't … well, I wasn't ready to think about that yet.

My mood and my smile only faltered when the doors opened on the lobby. Bobby and Eastman loomed by the exit like vultures.

"I'm sorry, Clay, but—" Bobby started before Eastman butted in and grabbed me by the elbow.

"Clayton Hart," he growled. "We're taking you in for questioning in regard to the murder of Jack Preswick."

***

Biometric scanners blinked at me from the room's four corners. Despite the tech, it looked the same way interrogation rooms have for centuries: nothing more than a concrete box with only a table and chairs to furnish it. It was hot, damp, and claustrophobic. As was traditional, I sat on one side, Bobby and Eastman on the other. We'd been at this all night, and I was losing patience.

"I don't know," I said for the umpteenth time.

"Fine, maybe you don't. But you're a clever one," Eastman said with a sneer. "Make a guess."

"Clever or not, Mama Hart didn't raise no daughters thick enough to make guesses in the company of detectives." I channeled her razor wit and unflinching pride. She *had* raised her daughters to not fold under pressure.

"Scanners say you're hiding something, Clay," Bobby said. My skin prickled. Sure, I was hiding all kinds of things: my heart ached for a dead partner, who also happened to be the reason I was stuck in this drowned city; my brain reeled trying to unravel the web of deceit I found myself wrapped up in; my flesh burned for the liar that had started it all. Plenty of telemetry for Bobby's scanners to take in.

"Everybody's hiding something in this town, Bobby," I said. "You oughta know that better than most." The rob's expression stayed as stony as his complexion.

"Look here, Hart," Eastman said. "If you've got evidence that you're keeping from us, I'll have you locked up for obstruction!"

Hot blood rose in my cheeks. I stood, slamming both fists into the tabletop. "You two have all but outright accused me of *two* murders, one of 'em my own partner," I snarled. Jack had been a pain in my ass, but he was *my* pain in the ass. "*Fragebak*, seems like you fellas are always sticking your nose in it and mucking up my business. As far as I can see, the best chance I have of clearing myself of the latest trouble you've caused me is bringing the murderers in myself. And the only way I can do that is by staying as far away from the two of you as I can. Now, if you want to go to the magistrate and tell her I'm obstructing justice, that's your business. But you better have something stronger than biometric telemetry to back you up. The last time you tried that we all had ourselves a good laugh. You wanna go around again? Go ahead—it's been a while since I took in a good show."

"Now, wait just—" Eastman started.

"And another thing," I said, jabbing my finger in his face, "I'm done with these little chats. You want to talk to me again, you better have enough to arrest me. Are we through?"

Bobby sighed. "We're through."

***

I stalked through the rain toward home. But around the corner from Rick's, my brooding was interrupted.

"Miss Hart?"

Collins. He stood in the alley beside the bodega that kept Jack awake at night.

I hurried to his side. "What are you doing here?"

He looked around suspiciously. "I got word that a dangerous man has arrived in Cibus City. I believe he is also after the briefcase."

"Got word?" I repeated. "From who—" I stopped and looked around myself. "Let's talk inside." I swept him around the corner, up the stairs, and into my apartment.

I sat on the bed, but Collins paced the small space. "Alright, let's have it," I said. "Who's this 'dangerous man'? The same one you and Moseby stole the briefcase from?" I wondered if it would be Florence's client or Greenstreet.

"In a manner of speaking. He hired us to find it. Marcus Greenstreet. But that's almost certainly a cover. The only name that has stuck with him is 'The Man in Black.'"

Fitting. "I've met with him." Collins didn't seem surprised. Nothing phased this man. And as much as that rankled, it was equally intriguing. Seductive, even. "He says you're a liar. Says you're the dangerous one."

"Who do you believe?"

"On that score?" I poured a pair of drinks and handed him one. "Both of you." I laughed. "But that's about all I believe. You ready to tell me about the briefcase?"

Collins sat down next to me and stared into his glass.

"Have you heard of the Hopperite Synthesizer?" he asked.

Of course, I had. The legend of the Hopperite Synthesizer was a favorite bedtime story across the Arm. "Remind me," I said anyway.

"The Hopperite Federation was a vast region with its central hub in the Melita Sector."

I whistled. "Melita's a long way from here."

Collins nodded. "Legend says they were far more advanced. But they mysteriously vanished about twelve millennia ago."

"Wasn't there something about a giant fish?"

"So the legends say," he said and smiled. "Whatever the case, they disappeared. But it's believed some of their technology survived. Specifically, a machine that can create anything out of thin air—food, clothing—"

"Weapons," I said. I finished off my Scotch and started to stand, but Collins took my glass and moved to the bottle himself.

He poured and looked out my window. With his back to me, he sipped from his glass and watched bioluminescent shapes dance in the methane outside. "Yes, weapons." He turned and handed me my glass. "But think of the good that could be done!"

"Greenstreet says you want to sell it." I emptied the glass in one gulp and handed it back. "That you aren't what you seem."

Collins smiled slightly. "And you believe him?"

"I've seen how fluid your story's been. Why should I trust you now?"

"Did he tell you why he wants it?"

I laughed. "He fed me some line about keeping it out of the wrong hands."

"The Man in Black is an agent of the Impound," Collins said, his voice flat.

The Impound.

Now, there was something to grant a moment's pause. Myths about the organization had persisted for centuries. Whenever new discoveries were made—especially involving alien technology—tales of the Impound's black-clad agents were sure to follow. It was said they confiscated research and left few credible witnesses in their wake. Could Greenstreet be one of them? The situation fit. If so, he was more dangerous than I thought. But he could also be my best opportunity.

"What about Flo—" My head swam. I hadn't had *that* much to drink.

"Don't worry about Florence. I can handle her." The room spun as he spoke. "Besides, she's just about too late. It's almost over."

"You ..." My limbs felt like lead. My eyelids drooped like they weighed ten pounds each. The bastard had *drugged* me. Adrenaline poured into my veins at the realization, and I grabbed at him. He easily batted my weakened hands away and I fell, helplessly, to the bed.

Fragebak.

"Yes. I'm sorry, Miss Hart. But it's time for me to go, and this was ... *easier* than the alternative. I like you, and I don't want to see you hurt. It's just a light sedative. I know, it comes on strong. But you'll be right as rain in a few hours, and I'll be far from here."

***

I awoke to a dark and empty apartment. My head ached and my mouth was dry. Greenstreet's eleven o'clock deadline was less than an hour away. And at that moment, I was out of the loop and empty-handed. I put my head between my knees and tried to make the room stop pinwheeling.

I missed Jack. He always had a way of coming up with odd little hunches at the most crucial moment. Damn him for leaving me alone on this.

I pulled on my overcoat and stepped out into the rain-soaked city. Through the window of the bodega around the corner, the holo-vision news blared. Jack hadn't been kidding about the volume; I could hear the broadcast half a block away.

"—*bringing the Union of Alderax and the Korganite Hegemony another step closer to interstellar war,*" the anchor's voice boomed. Her projected image loomed over the bodega's show window. "*And now, more on our developing local story,*" she continued. "*Uptown Cibus City was rocked this evening as the star-freighter* Zonbyt *exploded on the tarmac. Emergency crews were quick to contain the blast and prevent any structural damage to spaceport or city infrastructure. The* Zonbyt *was on her way home after her historic voyage as the first Union of Alderax vessel to travel to the Melita Sector in over a decade. With no volatile cargo listed on the manifest and the ongoing border dispute with the Korganite Hegemony, authorities suspect foul play. Altida Olvala, the* Zonbyt's *captain, is still unaccounted for …*"

I sprinted for the tubes to Uptown with a prayer of thanks to Jack on my lips before the anchor had a chance to finish her sentence.

But only steps from the bodega, I collided with a hunched shape that appeared from a blind alley. "*Fragebak*!" I spat as I nearly tripped over the object the vagrant had dropped.

A metallic briefcase.

My jaw popped like a broken hinge, and I stooped to help the figure up. This was no vagrant; the Alderaxian female, wearing the bars of a Merchant Captain on her collar, hunched and clutched her stomach. The downy feathers on her hands were stained olive with her blood. It seeped from a particle burn on her side. She struggled and reached for the briefcase, only to collapse into my arms once she had it.

"*Christ's blood!* Altida Olvala?" I asked. She clung to the briefcase like a life preserver as her eyes rolled. "Captain!"

Her short bill formed human words slowly and deliberately, careful to get them right. "Café Terra Firma," she whistled. "Clayton Hart."

"That's me!" I insisted. "That's—"

She was gone. Just a ragdoll in my arms.

I lowered Captain Olvala to the ground and, one by one, pulled her scaled fingers away from the case's handle. With the prize finally in my hands, I ran back the way I had come.

***

I stepped into my apartment empty-handed and found it much more crowded than when I had left. Greenstreet sat on the mattress and held Collins at gunpoint. Florence searched the room a second time.

"Ah, Miss Hart," Greenstreet said. "Right on time."

"Miss Hart, I—" Collins said.

I ignored him. For the first time since he had walked into Terra Firma, I was in control. All I had to do was keep it that way. Easy. Sure. "Ready to deal, Greenstreet?"

"May I presume that means you have my briefcase?" he said.

"I've got it." I poured a drink. "It's safe."

Florence snorted and trained her pistol on me. "She's left it with the barman downstairs. Let me—"

"Maybe Rick's got it, maybe he doesn't," I said. "But if you go down there with trouble on your mind, you'll find out why they call him 'Ray-Gun.'"

"No need for threats," Greenstreet said. "If Miss Hart has the briefcase, I am willing to deal." His voice was smooth. Calm. Completely in control. "What would you call an equitable price for a treasure like the legendary Hopperite Synthesizer?" He glanced around the cluttered apartment. "How does passage to the sector of your choice sound? And perhaps enough spoons to get you set up? Maybe enough to start a real detective agency? You've certainly got the chops for it."

My pulse quickened, but I kept my voice as smooth as Greenstreet's. "Sounds about fair. But there's a few things I'll need squared before I skip town."

"Miss Hart!" Collins said.

"For starters," I said, "why send Florence if you were going to make an offer yourself?"

Greenstreet smiled. "It seemed prudent to give you several paths to choose from. Not knowing what kind of woman you were, we couldn't be sure if money or righteousness would win the day."

Slick bastard. But I might have done the same.

"What about the murders?" I asked. "Jack Preswick, Franklin Moseby, and Captain Olvala?" Florence's lip twitched at their names.

"What of them?" Greenstreet said.

"Cops want me for one, maybe all. I don't need warrants chasing me across the Arm. I say we give 'em the merc."

Florence laughed. "Why don't we give 'em you? Or Collins?"

"I've got the briefcase, and you want it. A patsy's part of the price," I said to Greenstreet. I looked into Collins's too-perfect eyes. "If you think we can rig *him* up for the part, then let's talk. But at least if we give them Florence it has the benefit of being the truth. Mostly."

Florence sneered. She raised the pistol and stalked towards me. But before she could go more than a step, her face twisted in surprise. Greenstreet had jammed a jet injector into her thigh as she passed. As her body went slack and she fell to the floor, her gun clattered to my feet. I picked it up, and after a moment's consideration, handed it to Greenstreet. Collins gaped.

"You are remarkable, Miss Hart. Truly! One never knows what you'll do or say next!" Greenstreet chuckled and put both guns in his pockets. "Very well. She'll be out for a few hours now and you have your patsy. But if she should talk?"

"Who's gonna believe her?" I said. "Now, why'd she kill Moseby and Captain Olvala?"

"What does that matter?"

"Details, man." I drank and eyed Greenstreet. "The story we give the cops has to make sense." My heartbeat pulsed in my throat. This was the homestretch. I was moments from the truth, and better yet, a payday big enough to set me free of Cibus. I only had to *hold on.*

"You are indeed a clever one." Greenstreet smiled. "Franklin Moseby was an expert in Hopperite mythology. He, and his new assistant …" he said and looked at Collins. The man slumped to the floor, his handsome features dark. "… were funded by my organization in the hopes that they would make certain discoveries. However, when that eventuality finally occurred, the two ran. I was forced to pursue with my agent," he added, nodding to Florence.

"You didn't try to make a deal with Moseby?" I asked.

"Of course, I did! He refused. Too idealistic. Renée became … *agitated* … and made a poor decision." He wasn't too broken up about it. "As for Captain Olvala, when an Alderaxian freighter coming in from the Melita Sector arrived, we knew we had it. She was transporting the Synthesizer to the borders for Moseby and Collins. We went to meet with the captain, and who should we find there? Mr. Collins, of course. When the captain saw us, she fled. Renée took her shot, but Olvala evaded us. But there was really only one place she would go." He chuckled again. "If that's enough for you, Miss Hart, I'd like to see my briefcase now."

"How do I know you'll keep your end?" I asked.

"Have I yet lied to you? No," he said. "Concealed things for my own benefit, perhaps. Played things close to the vest, as they say. But I have not yet lied to you."

I looked from him to Collins, then opened my terminal. "Rick. That package? Bring it up."

***

Rick didn't keep us waiting. I answered his knock and found him with that ancient ray-gun strapped to his hip, the briefcase in hand, and a scowl etched on his face. "Everything all right, Clay?"

"We're fine, Rick," I said. "You can put that down on the desk."

Rick did as asked but stopped on his way out. "I'll be waiting for the all-clear," he said with a raised voice and a hand on the butt of his weapon. I nodded and closed the door behind him.

Greenstreet produced a thumb-sized fob from his suit coat and the briefcase unlocked with a click. The device inside was flat, with roughly ten square inches of surface area. A small panel to one side lit up at his touch.

The idea of it was fascinating. Something from nothing. Technology that could change the galaxy, for better or worse. Even Collins's demeanor changed. He stood and moved in for a better look.

"Let's give it a try, shall we?" Greenstreet said. He pulled a cylindrical bit of tech I didn't recognize from another pocket and waved it over the Synthesizer. "Herbal tea, please." There was a shimmer and a flash of light. When it passed, a glass of dark liquid sat where a moment before there was nothing. Greenstreet smiled and lifted the glass to his lips. But his expression soured at the first sip. "Gah!"

I took the glass and drank. It wasn't tea. It was alcoholic, and familiar. Almost like Scotch, but not quite. I drank it down. *Not bad.*

"Try something else," Collins muttered.

Greenstreet waved his wand again. "One particle-accelerating sidearm." Again, there was a shimmer and a flash, and again, a glass of dark liquid. "*Fragebak!*"

"It's not a food bank, an armory, *or* a prize to be sold." I laughed and took the fresh glass. "It's a minibar, and there's only one thing on the menu!"

Greenstreet was dumbfounded for only a moment. "Not every legend pans out, I suppose," he said with a smile. "Such is the nature of this business, after all. If you don't mind, Miss Hart, I'll be on my way now." He placed his wand on the Synthesizer and closed the briefcase.

"Now, hold on!" I protested. "We made a deal. I delivered my end. It's not my fault you didn't get what you bargained for."

He turned back, that frustrating smile still on his face. "I suppose you are entitled to some compensation. Here." He held out the brief-case. "This is of no real use to me. We know from experience Hopperite technology is too advanced to reverse engineer. Damn thing may as well be magic. Sell it as a novelty, keep it for yourself. I don't care." He put it down on the desk and left.

The instant the door latched behind him, I was on my terminal. "Bobby. You want the folks responsible for the *Zonbyt* as well as the murders of her captain and Franklin Moseby? Marcus Greenstreet and Renée Florence. Florence is out cold here at my place and Greenstreet just left with the murder weapon. If you hurry, you'll catch him." I closed the link before Bobby could question me and turned to my final loose thread.

Shaun Collins.

"Moseby was the only good one out of the lot of ya, wasn't he?" I asked.

Collins said nothing.

"Cibus is the only human way station between Melita, Earth, the Hegemony, and *the Union*. Moseby wasn't going to the Hegemony.

You were going to the Union. Meeting Captain Olvala here was your idea. You're a spy. A tanker the Alderaxians cloned up special for this mission," I said. "And *you* killed Jack."

"Got it all figured out now, Miss Hart?" he said.

"Not quite. Why kill Jack? Was it just to frame Moseby? To tie him up with the cops long enough for you to meet up with Olvala and make a break for the border without him?"

"Miss Hart. Clay—"

"But when Moseby turned up dead, too, you must have known your 'Man in Black' was here. That's why you came back. For protection. And maybe to use me as your own patsy. I got that right?"

His face was blank, and for the first time I was sure he was being honest. "The Hegemony is one excuse from declaring war on the Union. We don't have the resources to fight them for long." He sat on the bed. "This could have evened the odds. Now, who knows. I make no apologies for what I did—but—I am sorry it cost Mr. Preswick his life. What now?"

I sat next to him and looked into his eyes. Those beautiful, manufactured eyes. "Jack was a pain in my backside. He cost me my one way out of here. But you're supposed to look out for your partner." I sighed. "When something happens, you make it right. I have to make this right. For Jack." I hung my head. "I'll give you one hour, then I'm putting Bobby and his dipstick partner on your trail. One hour."

He leaned in and kissed me. "Thank you, Clayton." Then, like a shadow, he was gone.

I finished off the odd, almost-Scotch and picked up the briefcase. Leaving Florence locked in for Bobby to collect, I started down the stairs to Rick's.

My booth, and a new job, undoubtedly awaited.

NO MORE SECRETS

L.N. Hunter

I giggle when my turn at Truth or Dare comes. "Do you want to hear a secret?"

Four pairs of eyes look at me.

I don't know if it's the alcohol, or the weed, or something else, but a switch flips in my head, and I can suddenly hear *everything*. I can't believe I've been so deaf until now, until the whispers started. I struggle to contain my anticipation of how pleased everyone will be when I tell them.

"A secret..." I tease. "About Kerry..."

The others look at Kerry. I stare hard at her face, reading the subtle muscle contractions, the microexpressions, the furrowing brow—all blaring confusion.

But Kerry's perfectly clear to me. I can read her innermost thoughts.

"She's gay, and scared to tell anyone. But there's no need to be—I can help." I laugh. "There's no need to hide it," I tell her before turning to the others. "Kerry doesn't care about you, Mike, so stop wasting your time. She isn't wearing that tight skirt for you, mate. No, no, not at all."

Mike stares at me open-mouthed, while Kerry tries to deny it—I don't know why, since it's so obvious. Everyone surely suspected way before I spoke, but no one was brave enough to tell her. She looks like she might cry, but I'm not done yet. I know she'll feel better when I reveal what the others are hiding.

"It's all for Sonia, and Sonia doesn't even know. Sonia's so immersed in herself—it's true, it's true. She doesn't see what's going on around her. None of you do, but I can see all your secrets, all your ridiculous, unnecessary fears."

Spreading my arms, I repeat, "There's no need to hide."

I feel fantastic. Powerful. Invincible. The faces in front of me are twisted, but I hear the thoughts underneath their shouting. I can't understand why they're denying everything. I start to explain it's the truth and there's no point in running away from it.

Mike and Brian lever themselves out of the sagging sofa, hauling their unsteady bodies upright. I jump backwards, darting out of their reach.

"Brian likes wearing his mum's clothes," I add. "He believes he looks nice, but don't you think he needs to lose a bit of weight? And you, Mike, you're worried that your dick doesn't work. You tug and tug every night, but it's just not working. No wonder Kerry swings the other way. But don't worry, we all develop at different rates. It'll happen when it's right for you. Maybe you just haven't met the right person yet."

I discover that even though Mike's dick doesn't work, his fists certainly do. Brian's, too. I don't understand—my words are intended to help.

Two cracked ribs and a black eye. I end up missing a week of school.

***

On my first day back, I discover that Mike and Brian have been suspended. I barely notice their absence; I'm lost in the thoughts written on people's faces. The insistent whispers tell me more than I want to hear. I was helping my friends—my ex-friends—but they're all worse off than before I opened my mouth. I don't know what my new power's for, so I'm keeping what I can see and hear to myself for the moment.

In class, Ms. Simmons, our permanently scowling English teacher, drones on about how something-or-other is a metaphor for blah, blah, blah. I'm listening to what she says behind her words. Beneath her veneer of calm professionalism, the old cow hates us. I can tell, even though no one else sees it. She wishes each one of us was dead, even star pupil Jake, who aces every test. Ms. Simmons knows she's wasting her life here, spouting ideas she doesn't believe to students who don't care. She'd much rather be back in Paris with—it's difficult to make out his name—John? Jean? Johan? Moonlit Bateaux Mouches cruises on the Seine, picnicking at the Centre Pompidou fountains. Waking up in his bed.

She asks me a question and I stare blankly. The rest of the class laughs as I struggle to bring to mind what she's been talking about. The laughter booms in my ears, revealing even deeper secrets. I hear everything except the words Ms. Simmons is saying.

I spend the rest of the day in the same overloaded daze. The bus ride home is overwhelming.

Near the front, the laughing girl in the short skirt wants sex. It's the only thing that occupies her skull. She doesn't care who it's with as long as it happens soon. She thinks all her friends have lost their virginity—but I can tell they haven't. I've overheard them—I mean, heard with my ears, not with my superpower—either boasting about how good it was or drawling that it was nothing, really. They're lying to each other, because that's how society works: fit in with everyone else while simultaneously projecting an air of blasé superiority. They're even lying to themselves. But they can't lie to me. Behind their words and their smiles, I see desperation—their need to obliterate what they see as immaturity, yet all the time, they're drowning in fear and anxiety.

I clench and unclench my fists and screw my eyes shut, struggling to muffle their inner screaming. *Will it hurt? Will I enjoy it? Do I look normal? Can I do it right? What if my partner doesn't like it or tattles afterwards?* All this angst would evaporate if everyone had my new ability—they could see that they're all the same inside.

I wish I could show them, but that didn't work so well last time, for them or for me. Kerry and the others have been avoiding me since the party. I suppose I should be grateful that Mike and Brian haven't tried to beat me up again.

The laughing girl is flirting with an insecure boy who can barely read; all he has going for him are his wide, blue eyes and a lazy smile. He'd rather be at home, shooting zombies on his Xbox. I see his worries that no one will respect him, and that he's heading towards a dead-end job and alcoholism like his father.

I want to reassure him—to reassure them all—but I don't know how to.

At home, Mum asks how my day was, though I can tell she doesn't care. Every time I look at her now, I see she would rather I wasn't there. She longs to go somewhere far away—no more family, no waste-of-space husband and his distasteful nighttime groping and poking, no disappointing offspring. Choking back a sob as her casually dismissive gaze cuts deep into me, I tell her I've got a lot of studying to do and rush to my bedroom.

I can't concentrate—the detritus from all those other people's minds is racing around my head. Eventually, I push my books aside and go to bed. I toss and turn for most of the night, but somehow manage a little sleep. I'm still tired in the morning, but at least the only thoughts inside my head are my own.

I wish I could remain under the covers, hiding from everyone and their rampaging minds, but my pleas to stay home fall on deaf ears. Mum knows I'm faking an illness, and even drives me to school so that I have no opportunity to escape.

A skull-crushing migraine develops a few days later. An axe smashes into my head every time I catch a glimpse of someone, unable to prevent their secrets from running riot through my mind. I try not to look at people's faces and stare at the ground instead; concrete and gravel hide no anxieties. That makes things a bit better, except that I can't avoid instinctively peeking at people when I hear their voices and the unspoken messages hidden within their words.

I can't work out why I've got this power. I don't want it.

***

One Sunday, I hang back after church and ask Father Tate if I can have a moment of his time.

"What can I do for you… Kit, isn't it?"

"Father, why does God choose some people?"

He stares at me for a moment. "I'm not sure I understand what you mean."

"How does He decide who gets special gifts?"

His outward expression is one of confusion, but I see what he's thinking. I can see his desires. No, not the choristers, though he worries every time his glance lands on a child that someone might believe *that* about him. It's old Miss Armstrong, the organist. He's imagining himself doing her doggy style. She's eighty if she's a day, and one of the few people I can look at without my head exploding. She's got no secrets—gazing at her is quiet and calming. Soothing.

Apart from her, the world seems to be thinking about sex all the time. I suddenly realise that like her, I'm not. I have no desires, just this bewildering ability—it's not my fault that I see sex everywhere. I need to learn how to control my power, to empty my mind.

I have no one else to turn to, so I grit my teeth and try to unsee Father Tate's depraved coupling. I attempt to speak again, but can't find the right words and have to make do with, "I can… see things. Is it something God's given me?"

He frowns at me, his face tightening. Does he know what I can see inside him? "Kit, we all have unique gifts. It's the duty of every one of us to use them as best we can."

"How do I do that, Father?" I plead, reaching for his hand. "I don't understand what I need to do."

He disengages his hand, fearful to be seen touching a young person. "We should strive to better ourselves and humanity in everything we do. It's our duty to God and to each other." He seems to realise that his trite homilies are no help, then leans forward, conspiratorially. "If something is troubling you, Kit, and you don't feel comfortable talking to your parents, I can listen to anything you want to tell me, though I'm not used to"—he laughs self-consciously—"giving advice to … younger people. I'm sure I have the phone number of someone who might be able to help if you need more than I can offer. It's all private and confidential, so you don't have to worry."

I stare at his face. Behind the banal sympathy, a sudden clarity snaps into place.

Father Tate may not have any answers in his spoken words, but I know what I must do now, thanks to the whispers beneath them. Visible over his shoulder, the patterns of coloured light shining through the stained glass windows paint my path. I sense a higher power communicating with me, pulsing through my soul. I inhale deeply, breathing in my new knowledge.

As I leave Father Tate to his lustful dreams, the echo of my footsteps on the marble floor tells me what to do. The quiet calmness of the empty churchyard beyond the doors tells me what to do.

God tells me what to do.

In His wisdom, He's granted me His purity and the ability to see people's innermost desires. He's given me immunity to those desires within myself, so that I am able to sort humanity into the good and the corrupted. To be judge and jury.

And, He commands, *to mete out punishment.*

I skip school the following morning and head into the city with a kitchen knife in my pocket. It has cut through the cloth, and the cool metal rests against my leg. The unyielding blade creates an insistent pulse on my skin, beating in time with the pounding in my head.

Propping myself against a wall opposite the train station entrance, I watch commuters file out. Looking at them drives spikes through my eyes, but I force myself to stare at each one. A few are quiet, like Miss Armstrong, and my gaze slides away from them. I have to focus on the ones God wants me to take note of. The ones internally vibrating with hatred and loathing.

A bald man with a contented grin on his face strides out of the station. Behind his placid façade, he's thinking about his profits. Damn the cheap labour, the zero contract workers, the corners cut, the tax dodging, and the lies upon lies upon lies. But I can hear him screaming. He doesn't care about his company's working conditions, or how his employees live on the pittance he doles out. However, he does like how Tony and Carol give him 'extra favours' for a few quid. Both so young and so... accommodating. He doesn't have them round to his house—my goodness, what if the wife discovered his weakness? A few grubby minutes in the storeroom has to suffice.

I push myself up from the wall and follow him to his workplace. All the time, Baldy's imagination is a cesspool of dreams about what he'll do to Tony later that day, and my head throbs. Sweat drips into my eyes, and I have to keep blinking to clear them. He walks towards a small, neat building tucked under a road bridge. I can't tell what business he does here—the faded sign above the door won't come into focus—but it's the sort of place that hides him from inquisitive eyes.

He unlocks the door, and throwing it wide, enters his pokey office. I slide in before the spring closes it behind him.

He shuffles some papers on his desk for a moment before he notices me standing just inside the door.

"Who are you?" he barks.

I can't tell if his voice is angry or confused—I can barely hear him over his shouting mind. Behind his eyes, he's forgotten about Tony, and is thinking about my youthful body.

I freeze. I no longer know what to do. Everything seemed clear before, but now, in the same room as this man and his festering mind, I can't do what I need to.

Each thud of my heart tightens a band around my skull. I can't breathe. I can't think.

Baldy takes a step closer. The room shakes, and I stumble and almost fall.

He says something, but I can't hear it over the screaming in my mind.

Suddenly, somehow, the knife is in my hand.

Baldy's eyes dart towards it and then back to my face. He pales and licks his lips. "What do you think you're doing?"

The knife's been warmed by my body, and the blade is eager to get to work. Its heat spreads up my arm and starts to ease the pressure in my head. I pull myself upright and advance.

"Get away!" the man shrieks, but I surge forward without conscious thought and plunge the knife into his stomach. I press hard, up into his heart, not letting him escape, as hot wetness gushes over my fingers.

His arms flap, and his mouth opens and closes, then he slithers to the floor. The knife, my hand still wrapped around it, slips out as he falls. He gasps twice and stops moving. Stops screaming his sordid secrets at me.

Silence.

I stare at his body as I force mine to relax. My heavy breathing subsides, and my mind becomes quiet. The throbbing in my skull has receded, replaced with a warm comfort I don't think I've ever experienced before. Killing him was much easier than I expected; I didn't have to think—it all came quite naturally. Confirmation that what I'm doing is right. A sign that God approves. I wipe the knife and my hand on his jacket. The blade seems to sigh as I slide it back into my pocket. Sated, it throbs in satisfaction against my skin.

I'm able to go to school for the rest of the week. I feel almost normal. No secrets batter my mind for days. After a time, however, the glow fades, and the pressure builds inside my skull again. I need to go out again the following week to find someone else deserving of God's punishment.

And the week after.

***

I've killed a dozen people now—no, not people. I've rid the world of a dozen loathsome creatures who aren't entitled to the gift of life. Some of their deaths get a few minutes of sensationalist coverage on the news, but there's no mention of their impulses, as if everyone is too scared to admit that society is rife with these creatures' vile wickedness. And there is no mention of me; God is protecting His servant.

Then my ability directs me to a woman, a cheat and a liar.

I follow her to her flat and let my knife do its job once again. As I stand panting, surveying my handiwork, I hear a cry from another room. Peering through the door, I see a toddler standing up in his cot. He stares at me. Perhaps I should have seen that she was a single mother and passed over her, despite her sins. The notion briefly crosses my mind that God made a mistake, but that can't be possible. What can I do now? I don't want to, but I have to kill the child. It's my duty, God tells me.

Things change after that. Wherever I go, people stare back, as if they're unpeeling my skin and looking at what's underneath. As if they've acquired my ability, too. They don't like what they see. Sure, some of them pretend to be my friend, asking if everything's OK, offering—with phony concern on their faces—to listen to anything I want to tell them. I know they're trying to trick me.

They want my secrets for themselves.

I'm confused. God gave me this power to do good, but now He's working against me. Is this because I doubted Him?

I need to fix it. I need to prove my faith.

I need to kill them all.

THE GRAVEKEEPER

Faraz Rezai

The gravekeeper awoke at dawn, as he had done for many long and unfathomable years past, to the tattered ceiling of his crooked hut. With weary hands, he lifted himself from where he lay, the aged wooden boards of the bedframe groaning as he fumbled for a pair of thin spectacles. He yawned silently, stretching his arms above his head, then, marked with the dogged intent of a man emburdened by habit, made for the crooked sink in the corner of the room. He stooped to fill a hollow bucket, bare feet shuffling against unfurnished stone, and once the bucket brimmed and swayed with icy water, he made slowly for the hunched door which separated the peeling walls of his hut from the rest of the barren grove.

The gravekeeper was a pale and feeble man, his features worn by years of lonely service. He paused a second as he reached the open door, two grey and lifeless eyes scanning the grove. Silence and inertia stretched before him, just as they had the morning before, but something in that sight must have appeased the old man for he set forth without hesitation upon his pilgrimage. As he stumbled through the grove, carrying nothing but the bucket of brimming water which he clung tightly to his breast, his tattered hair swayed madly in the breeze and the creased skin of his weathered face pulled tight. He may once have been a tall man, but the arch of his back was so painfully severe now that he could almost taste the earth as he jolted forwards.

The ancient necropolis to which the gravekeeper had prescribed his home was wholly forgotten to the rest of the world. In all his years in service to the crumbling tombs, he had yet to witness another soul setting foot upon the land. The bare and desolate trees were entirely devoid of birdsong, and even the worms seemed to have disappeared from the rotting soil. But rather than discourage him, this very fact spurred the gravekeeper on, and had perhaps even inspired his initial migration to the grove all those years ago.

As the old man came finally upon the first of the aged and crumbling teeth which jut out, slanted from the earth, he knelt and bowed his head, placing the heaving bucket softly beside the grave. The light from the morning sun was harsh, and the grove's autumnal winds beat upon him with cold and bitter persistence, but nothing could deter his withered hands from performing those solemn rites to which he had enshrined his life. He dipped his bare hands into the cold water of the bucket, and brought them gently to rest upon the etched and rugged stone. With reverent strokes, he washed the grime from the aged cenotaph, his gnarled fingers seeming to soften as they scraped away the dust and dirt.

Once the first of the crumbling monuments glimmered brightly in the harsh autumn sun and the decaying leaves had been cleared from the soil, the gravekeeper picked up his heaving bucket and moved onto the next. At each new grave, his tender gaze would pause a second upon the fractured carvings which may once have amounted to an epitaph before kneeling to perform his solemn ritual. In spite of his reverence, the old man had never once wondered at the identity of those forgotten souls who rested beneath his feet. Man, woman, or child. Peasant, diplomat, or king. In death, they had all been renounced and forsaken by the world, and were, as such, deserving of hi s care.

The deeper into the grove he travelled, the more ancient and strange the tombstones became. The traditional crosses and crucifixes of the Christian burial grounds slowly gave way to bulging slabs of Roman marble, complete with the Latin characters of some disfigured and long deceased dialect. With the same dutiful reverence, the gravekeeper repeated his ritual upon these marble shrines, kneeling solemnly before the crumbling stones and carving away the filth. The further he travelled, the further the blazing sun would sink in the midafternoon sky, but the lightening load of his bucket and the purified stones left in his wake helped spur him forwards.

Even further beyond the marble shrines, where the branches of hollow trees pointed ghastly and forewarning fingers, the tombs became stranger and more ancient still. Here, twisted monoliths of early limestone ravaged the earth, protruding from the soil as monstrous jaws inscribed with symbols of the old Celtic tribes. These limeston e effigies littered the ground in isolated clumps, where the different clans had undoubtedly marked their distinctions, but to the gravekeeper and to the passage of time, no distinction remained. He knelt here with the same stoic reverence, peeling away hardened mud from twisted limestone until every tomb in the ancient grove had been cleansed and attended.

As he cleared away the crumbling leaves from the final limestone grave, he looked up to the sky. In his devotion, he had failed to notice the encroaching darkness. A veiled moon peered over a bleak and desolate sky, as the cold howling of the wind did anything to atone for the eternal silence which surrounded him. There was once a time when the gravekeeper would have returned to his hut before the blazing sun had completed its cycle, but with the passing years, his hands had grown tired. Regardless, there remained water in the bucket for one final tribute, and with unfaltering step, he stumbled forward, ever deeper into shadow, wherein lay that final archaic monument which denoted the end of his sacred journey.

Deep in the furthest recesses of the ancient grove, upon that desolate and gloom-ridden hill which even the shadows dared not touch, he arrived upon the decayed ruins of his final shrine. In its time, it must have been a wondrous relic: a sprawling mausoleum of lustrous stones which spanned the full expanse of the slopes on which it rested. Great spiralling monoliths of magnificent and unutterable architecture once clawed their way from the earth here, the many elements which comprised their structure now long forgotten to the fleeting memories of man.

But as the gravekeeper descended upon those ancient ruins—those primordial ruins which predated the essence of time itself—there remained barely a vestige of that once proud and magnificent glory. With the passage of aeons immemorial, the great and shining spires had been reduced to dust, and the stones which comprised them devoured by the roaring winds. Only the centrepiece itself remained, the opening to an archaic crypt of strange and unfathomable design, uniquely preserved amid an ocean of solitude and decay.

As he reached the opening, the old man took a moment to look back over the ancient cemetery he had just traversed. A peculiar quality of stillness had consumed the grove. The howling winds were suddenly silent, and the moon had retreated behind a hazy mist of black clouds. In the ensuing darkness, there remained no trace of the path he had followed. All that remained as he looked about him was his lonely perch atop that gloom-ridden hill, and the time ravaged crypt beneath h im.

He wiped his brow and tightened his grip on the bucket. The air felt colder than usual. Reaching down, he raised the opening, revealing a set of crumbling stairs which burrowed deep into the earth. A vast chasm of impenetrable darkness. Slowly, groping tentatively at the half-eroded stones which composed the walls of the staircase, he began to descend into that darkness wherein lay the final burial site of the ancient necropolis, and the apotheosis of his voyage.

Over the years, the gravekeeper's eyesight had grown accustomed to the dim light of the buried stairway, but this night yielded an incomparable challenge. The veiled moon and starless sky did nothing to illuminate his path, and as he climbed further into the bowels of the earth he could barely make out the obscure silhouette of his own shuffling feet. With every step the stones felt colder, and the remaining water splashed pitifully against the hollow bucket. Although he could not see, the gravekeeper knew precisely where he was, for his withered lips numbered each and every step. Ninety-three, ninety-four, nin-ety-five. With heaving breaths, he drew deeper into the chasm, until finally the stones evened out beneath his feet, and the narrow staircase yawned into a small, low-hanging chamber.

As with the halls of Tartarus, not even a vestige of light was permit-ted an audience this night in the ancient crypt. A primordial darkness consumed and unified the senses, blurring the path ahead with the path of return, as the old man fumbled forward with unwavering spirit. Several steps forward, one back, and a few to the right, before the gravekeeper found the head of the raised sarcophagus to which this crypt, and perhaps even the entire cemetery, were tribute to.

To describe the sarcophagus even in perfect light would have been a challenging feat. A large, oblong tomb of strange and bewildering geometry, etched with cyclopic patterns which resembled nothing known to man. It was both elegant and crude. Deep ridges of fascinating shape and proportion embellished the outer edges of the stone casket, a possible affliction of the passing aeons. But it was near impossible to pinpoint exactly where the decay of time had begun, and where the strange designs surpassed imagination.

As the old man rested a hand on the cold stone of the ancient slab, a gentle wave of calm passed through his body. Though all the cemetery's monuments were equal in the gravekeeper's eyes, when he had first stumbled upon this crypt buried deep in the heart of the necropolis, it had aroused his fascination like no other—not so much for its strangeness than its seclusion. He fell to his knees and got to work, dipping his hands into what remained of the water before tracing the clefts and grooves of the tomb with reverent fingers. He knew the clefts of the timeworn stone like the clefts of his own palms, and he needed neither moon nor stars to perform his duty.

In that all-pervasive darkness, the old man became one with his work. Wiping away the little dirt which dared disrupt such timeless slumber, his soft knees pressed deeper into the ancient earth. Slender hands slid against cold stone, following its contours and grooves in an elegant dance of devotion. The flickering movements of the gravekeeper's fingers were unconscious and innate, dictated by something beyond himself, as he slowly melted together with the tomb. For but a fleeting moment, he felt as one with the stone, unable to tell where his fingers ended and the elements began. But almost as soon as the transfixion took him, his work was done, and the trance was broken.

With a glimmer of sadness in his eyes, the old man arose, ready to depart the ancient crypt and return to his tattered hut across the grove. But as he fumbled forward for the crooked staircase which would lead him back into the starless night, the empty bucket slipped from his grasp, rolling beneath his outstretched feet. With nothing to grasp at in the darkness, he lurched forward violently, his head striking something cold and hard on the way down.

In the singular second that it took for the old man to meet the ground, he was overcome by a sudden flash of lament. His eyes began to dizzy and spin, as images long buried in the winding corridors of his mind drifted to the surface. A small farmhouse on soft country hills. The laughter of children beside a warm hearth. Overwhelming impressions of tragedy and remorse. Of a bitterness which stained the mind. A piercing pain, long thought forgotten, impaled his heart once more, as the memories of a lifetime long deceased were swiftly replaced by another: one spent in solitude and repentance.

For how many silent moments he remained outstretched upon the muddied earth, the gravekeeper did not know, but as he laboured to return to his feet, something about the buried chamber felt changed. He realised that though distinct, faint shapes had materialised in the darkness. He could see the etched stone walls which enveloped him, and the crumbling staircase to his right, spiralling up and out of sight. Before him were the obscure edges of the ancient sarcophagus to which he had just tended, and behind the sarcophagus, a dim and ethereal glow.

A gentle presence filled the room, emanating from the heart of the light, and as the old man leaned forwards to discern the shadows before him, a second wave of light flooded the ancient chamber. In the newfound brightness, the soft silhouette of a tall and spectral figure was revealed, hooded and clad in strange and flowing robes. The figure's eyes locked upon those of the gravekeeper. Pools of bright obsidian. Beneath the hood were a set of pronounced and archaic features: rough and calloused skin, as hard as the stone tomb over which it presided; a long, slender nose; a pair of dark, sunken lips. A primeval essence emanated from the figure's shimmering form, and yet its presence instilled a ubiquitous calm about the room. Beneath the hood, the figure's lips were drawn in the shape of a warm and welcome smile, and the gravekeeper found himself mesmerized by a peculiar sense of beauty.

Almost instantly, he felt a kinship with the apparition, and as it lifted a twisted finger towards the crumbling stairs, the old man instinctively followed its command. As he began the long climb back to the surface, not once did he turn to check behind him, for he could feel the gentle presence of the spectral figure following patiently behind. A warmness filled the old man's soul as he followed the winding tunnel, the path before him this time illuminated by all directions.

As he emerged from the opening to the crypt, he noticed that the dark clouds had parted, revealing a host of glistening stars. Among them was a brilliant full moon, lighting up the midnight sky and enveloping the cemetery in a soft, silver haze. Upon his perch atop the hill, the old man could see everything: the pale grass dancing gently in the sweet autumn wind; the ghostly trees whistling serenity to the borders of the grove; and between them, stretching as far as the eye could see, legions of lonely and forsaken tombs glimmering in the spectral light.

But the tombs were lonely and forsaken no longer, for emerging out of the silver haze was an ocean of shimmering forms. Some stood proud and tall, while others slithered and crawled across the earth. Some wore crowns and jewels and priestly robes, while others were draped in tattered linens. The faces of some were scarred and burnt, while others beamed softly in the moonlight. But all, without exception, bore warm and healthy smiles upon their lips, welcoming the gravekeeper to their midnight grove.

The old man turned to face the shimmering figure who had followed him from the crypt. Their eyes met, and in those obsidian pools he saw it all. A quality of cosmic assurance, and a permeating warmth which encompassed the night. The old man had never felt such comfort and kinship as he did in that singular moment, and as his tears flooded the starlit earth, the ancient figure spoke in a strange and eldritch tongue.

"You are bound no longer."

He raised a shimmering finger, pointing past the ephemeral shadows to where the silver haze met distant hills. The silhouette of a small farmhouse faded into view, as the laughter of children mingled with the scent of strawberries in the breeze. And on the porch of the farmhouse, flickering brightly, was a great hearth, beckoning the old man forwards. A sudden exhilaration filled the old man's heart, and he set off for the distant hills, gliding past the shining tombs and glimmering shapes which bowed their heads in reverence. He grew taller and stronger with every step, the pains and aches of time suddenly forgotten as he raced through the night.

But as his form gave way to shadow, the depths of the earth betrayed a second truth. Buried in an ancient crypt deep within the cemetery, the mangled body of an aged gravekeeper kept the remains of a bygone tomb company. With skull shattered by cold stone and limbs soaked in blood, a pair of vacant eyes searched for the light of stars they would never see. And upon those eyes, set in their eternal slumber, the first specks of dust had already begun to settle.

PLENTY
Julia Rylen

One

New York City, A.D. 2042

They had been burning books that day.

The act no longer disgusted her. It was an old wound now, one of many, the least of a myriad of tiny cuts she'd become accustomed to. In the end, it was no different than the poisoned rain.

Just another bit of acid to numb her.

The day everything changed, they had foraged in the farthest, oldest section of the library, dragging ancient, dusty hardbacks from their shelves and flinging the volumes into their rusted Radio Flyer. Stacking them neatly would have been more efficient, but throwing the books helped her forget they were priceless.

"Enough?" Jacob asked.

Leia bobbed her head in agreement and he turned away to convince the cart to follow. It wobbled over the tile floor of the main aisle in protest as they made their way toward the doors facing Fifth Avenue.

"The wheel's gonna go," she said.

"It'll hold."

The squeak of the misshapen axel swallowed her reply. Jacob didn't deserve her pessimism, anyway.

She darted from the wagon to blow a fleeting kiss to Patience and Fortitude. The marble lions on the steps of the library were showing signs of decay, and somehow that bothered her nearly as much as using books to keep the winter's chill at bay.

By the time they reached the condo—not theirs before The Trouble began, of course, but as good as theirs now—evening threatened.

They hefted the load up three flights of stairs, and Jacob guided the cart's front wheels over the threshold of their front door. His wrists caught her eye.

"Leia?"

She dragged her gaze to his face, unable to respond. When had he gotten so thin?

"Start the fire while I fill the bucket?"

She nodded and shuffled to the makeshift hearth, watching until Jacob disappeared toward the kitchen. Keeping her eyes on the doorframe, she grabbed a book from the pile, dismembering it with ease.

Rip.

Pages fluttered down onto thirsty flames, blackening and contorting in death. Leia couldn't have said how many she'd fed to the fire while staring toward the kitchen, willing Jacob to return.

They hadn't much food, but tonight, they'd be warm.

Rip. Rip.

Her hand gripped the next book, automatically splaying it open to tear the pages more easily from the binding. The paper resisted as if digging in its heels. Frowning, she snapped it closed and turned it over in her hands. *Plenty: A Witch's Book of Wishes* stared back at her.

With a bitter laugh, she tossed the entire book into the firebox.

After Jacob returned with the water, he filled the kettle carefully, the last of the tiny apples bulging from his jacket pocket. He sat down next to her at the hearth and held them out for her to take. "I've had enough," he said with the same crooked smile he always gave her. "Take them both."

***

Hunger awoke Leia in the deep, silent dark. Jacob slept beside her, curled in against the cold. She forced herself to rise—if only to encourage the fire with more books—wrapping a scarf around her neck against the chill.

Alongside the ashes lay *Plenty*, its cover mangled and buckled from heat. She drew it out, wiping the soot away with her glove.

It fell open, revealing a marred page. On it, instructions, recorded by an ancient hand.

You may conjure necessities with undivided, unblemished paper. Simply write the need in red ink; if you write the need once, you will receive enough. If you write the need more than once, you will receive plenty.

You may write up to three different necessities on the paper, but they must be alike in some way.

Speak the words necessitates meas de heri adducere *over the paper. Turn the paper over. Repeat the word* praesterno *three times. Fold it, obscuring the words.*

Note: this spell may only be performed thrice within a lifetime. Most importantly, ensure that you do not

The rest of the instructions had been consumed by flame.

Leia didn't know why, but she freed the page from the cover and placed it in her pocket, stoked the fire, and went back to bed.

New York City, A.D. 2027

A breeze ripples over the sidewalk, escorting the early morning commuters to the subway station at Seventy-seventh and Lexington with a promise of spring's first warm day. It flows down the street until sweeping over an open trash receptacle, dislodging a page that looks like it had been ripped from a book.

The paper tumbles down the cement, encouraged by the wind until it comes to rest against the shoe of a man waiting for his ride just steps from his home.

People are gross, the man thinks as he frowns at the paper. *They can't even bother to use trash receptacles the city provides.* Since it looks clean enough, he reluctantly picks it up.

The man's cell phone vibrates—apparently, his Uber is delayed at the traffic light at Seventy-second and Park. *Probably some idiot tourist blocking the corner. I'll be late getting to work, which means I'll be late getting home—again. Becca's going to go off the rails, as usual.*

The paper in his hand has an odd quality to it; somehow, it looks both old and new. Its one ragged side—as if it had been torn out of a binding—seems to glow with thick, black shadow. Intrigued, the man unfolds the heavy paper, revealing handwritten words.

Tomatoes

Corn

Strawberries

The three words cover the entire page, as if the would-be author was trying to memorize their spelling by writing them over and over again.

All of that for some maniac's dumb-ass grocery list.

The man crumples the paper and tosses it toward the trash bin. It misses. A stranger walking by pushing a baby carriage catches his eye in silent judgment but doesn't stop to rectify the man's botched shot.

I'm just not ready to push one of those around, no matter how many times Becca begs. I'm sure I'll hear about that tonight, too. Maybe I can put her off another year, if I play my cards right.

A breeze blows the paper back toward his shoe. The man bends over and retrieves the wad of paper from the sidewalk once more.

A small, black sedan pulls up and an Uber driver leans out the driver's side window. "Isaac?"

The man nods. Grumbling, he stuffs the paper into the pocket of his coat before getting into the Uber. *Weird,* he thinks, *Becca picked up those exact things from Cali's Bodega yesterday. Wouldn't it be funny if this was her list?*

Ten hours later, he yanks open the stainless steel door of his refrigerator, only to gape at the space where the tomatoes, corn, and strawberries had been that morning.

New York City, A.D. 2042

A scream rent the oily air.

Leia jumped, upending one of their last two glasses. Precious water—painstakingly distilled several hours before—darkened the wooden kitchen table. She snatched the glass before it rolled off the table and bolted to the door.

Jacob was standing with his back to her, frozen, garden gate held open by his hand.

"What's wrong? What happened?"

He didn't move.

"Jacob?"

Her husband sank to his knees.

She could see beyond him now.

The rooftop garden was overflowing with plants—tomatoes, corn, and strawberries—ripe, fully grown, and perfect.

***

"But that's not how the universe works, Leia," Jacob said, shaking his head. "Things do not simply appear out of thin air. They must have come from somewhere else. Someone must have planted them in the garden overnight."

They were sitting at the kitchen table in mismatched chairs, three chipped bowls overflowing with tomatoes, corn, and strawberries perched between them. The stain from the spilled water was still visible in the wood like a dark ghost of the past, watching.

"Do you hear what you're saying?" he pressed.

"I know. It sounds ridiculous. But there's no other explanation." She shrugged. "It doesn't look like they were just planted. The dirt around the plants is packed and the—"

Jacob cut her off. "I agree."

"And why would someone do that? The only access to the roof is through this condo."

"I know."

They stared at the harvest, shaking from hunger, equal parts giddy and suspicious, words useless.

"I made a list," she said softly.

Jacob's brow furrowed but he kept his gaze on the bowls as if he couldn't bear to look away. "A list?"

"A shopping list. Remember when we used to make lists before going to the grocery store?"

Jacob glanced at her uncertainly then fixed his eyes on the bounty.

"One of the books I put in the fire didn't burn completely," Leia said. "There was one page left with writing on it—only part of a page, really. There were instructions on how to do it."

"How to make a grocery list?"

"No. How to conjure things you need," she said.

Jacob frowned, harder this time. "Conjure? Like a magic trick?"

"It said you can only write three different things—similar things—so I wrote them over and over. Maybe that's why there's so much. I tried to pronounce the words, too. I thought ..." Leia stopped. "I didn't think it would work."

"I found a pen back in the drawer here," she continued. "I ... I used a blank page from the same book." She sighed. "One of three that were stuck to the back cover. I was just playing around, thinking about things I used to eat, wishing having food was as easy as buying some at the grocery store. I didn't expect ..."

She let the spoiled air steal her thought.

Together, they stared at the bright red and yellow anachronisms.

Jacob said nothing for a long time.

"I'll try one," he said finally.

She reached out to pluck a fat strawberry from the bowl. "I can, too—"

"Wait," he said.

Leia frowned. "I—"

"I should try one first in case something is wrong. I don't want you to get sick," Jacob said. "It's prudent."

"Prudent," she echoed.

Jacob slowly bit into a fruit, nostrils flaring. His eyes slid closed.

And he began to laugh.

New York City, A.D. 2027

"What did you do with the strawberries?" Becca calls from the kitchen as she ducks her head into the fridge. "Where are they?"

"No idea," the man says as he bends and ties his shoe.

At least last night's discussion had ended in agreement: she conceded to wait another year, and he conceded to her choice of names should the child be a boy. He still can't tell if she was teasing him or not. The choice suggested by the names of the Patriarchs in the Torah seems obvious. Cliché. Pedestrian, even.

She could change her mind. There is plenty of time.

Shoes tied, the man takes his coat from the hall closet. As his hand searches the pocket for his sunglasses, his fingers touch the wrinkled grocery list he'd found on the sidewalk instead.

He ducks into the hall bathroom and presses the creases flat but finds nothing written on either side.

"Becca," he calls, frowning, as he crumples the paper into a ball. "I'm leaving now."

There's no response from the kitchen.

The man flings the paper into the garbage can and bolts the front door behind him.

Two

New York City, A.D. 2042

Leia brought *Plenty's* two remaining blank pages and the pen to the kitchen table. The spill had long since dried, leaving an outline of white chemical crust.

Some things could not be boiled away.

The tomatoes, corn, and strawberries didn't last. They were not like apples, hardy and stout in the hard winter; they were fleeting and fragile and bruised easily, fussy as newborns. Even though they had wrapped what remained after they'd eaten their fill in soft linen, barely any survived past the third day.

The plants, however, withered the night they had appeared from thin air.

We'll keep the seeds, Jacob had assured her.

The empty sheet of paper lay between them, waiting.

"Don't wish for more food," Jacob said.

"Why not?"

"We need to think about this differently," he said, leaning back into his chair. "If we had something else—say, gold—we could do whatever we wanted, go wherever we wanted. Buy whatever we wanted."

She nodded.

"We could get a farm along the Southern Shore. Everyone says it's better there. Richer soil. Longer summer. Crops are easier to grow. People there have plenty."

"Rumors," she scoffed.

"Maybe."

They stared at the blank page.

She began to write, her fingers clumsy with cold.

New York City, A.D. 2027

"Card's declined."

"Excuse me?"

"Your card. It was declined," the clerk says, annunciating each word as if the man has trouble hearing. "Got another way to pay?"

As she waits for him to reply, she snaps her gum and parks her hand on her hip clearly stating *she doesn't have all day*.

"I...uh, sure. Must be something wrong..." The man digs in his wallet for another card. "Here."

She straightens her shirt and runs the one he offers. She rolls her eyes then looks him up and down, her gaze catching on his silk tie. "This one, too. Declined."

"I'm not sure what's happening," the man says lamely.

She drags his groceries back across the counter toward the register. "Sorry," she says. She doesn't sound it.

"Do you have an ATM?" he asks.

She points with her chin, her arm still wrapped around his would-be purchase. "Back left corner near the bathrooms."

When the man pulls out his debit card from his wallet, a paper falls out and floats to the floor. He picks it up. It matches the other one—the maniac's grocery list—in color and texture. This one is folded to match the size of a credit card.

On it, in the same strange hand, is written *gold*. Over and over and over.

He places his debit card in the ATM and goes through the motions of accessing his accounts.

All his balances are zero.

New York City, A.D. 2042

Leia stumbled to the hearth to heat the last of the water distilled the evening before. Even after all the years since The Trouble, she could still convince herself that if the water was warm, she was drinking tea.

After setting the kettle, she yanked up the floorboard where Jacob hid the very last of their food.

Two desiccated corn cobs were perched on a mound of coins, glistening in the squalid daylight.

Three

Southern Shore, A.D. 2042

"It's not far," Jacob said. "Just over the next rise."

They'd been walking for eight days, foraging as they went, slowed by the heavy Radio Flyer laden with coin. At that moment, the gold was as much a blessing as a burden, for the wagon needed attention daily. It was only a matter of time before they would be unable to repair i t.

But the weather was warm—warmer than they've felt in months, and the air sweeter, somehow.

Hope filled their bellies.

When they saw the gate to the Southern Shore towering in the distance, Jacob scouted around to find a place to bury the better part of their gold. He piled the remainder in a threadbare backpack.

"When we get there, I'll do the talking," he said, hauling the pack onto his shoulder. It strained against the weight of the treasure inside. "I'll petition for entry at the gate. Remember, if they ask, you're a nurse with exceptional gardening skills. I may have to slip the guard a coin or two. Either way, make sure you seem friendly, but not too friendly. After we're admitted, I'll ask to see the proconsul."

"And you? What are you?"

"A carpenter. No, an architect."

"Sounds important," Leia said.

"Maybe I'll say I was in construction. Yeah, that'll be better." Jacob picked up his pace. "Imagine! Land of our own. Community protection. Potential for trade ..." He shook his head. "It's almost too good to be true."

Silently, she tucked the remaining blank page from *Plenty* into her right sock.

***

They reached the gate an hour before sunset.

"Names?" the guard intoned, looking them up and down as the two stood, quietly, motionlessly. Another loomed a few feet away, cleaning a rifle. A third leaned against the gate, casually cleaning the space under his fingernails with a hunting knife.

"Leia and Jacob Rubin," Jacob said.

"Residence before The Trouble?"

"We lived in upstate New York, but moved back to Manhattan after everything went down. We wanted to find my parents—"

The man cleaning the gun snickered.

"We're New York City, born and raised," Jacob added. "Both of us. My parents lived at Seventy-eighth and—"

"We don't care about cities here," the one with the knife said.

Jacob swallowed. "Right."

"Are you carrying weapons?" the first guard asked.

"No, sir."

"Then what's in that backpack of yours? Looks heavy," he continued. Slowly, Jacob took off the pack and slid the zipper part way open for the man to see.

"We'd like to inquire as to whether you have land for sale," Jacob said.

After a glance inside the pack, the guard nodded at his companions. The two stalked over and began to frisk Jacob and Leia aggressively.

"Is that so?" said the first guard with a smile that didn't touch his eyes.

***

Leia and Jacob were blindfolded and taken past the gates and led down what felt like a dirt path. Eventually, they were ushered into a building and ordered to sit. When a guard removed their blindfolds, they found themselves in an office inside a log cabin—sparse but clean, new, and warm. Leia could still smell the spruce they'd felled to build it.

A wiry man, lounging behind an oak desk, folded his hands and stared at them for a moment before speaking. "I am Proconsul Edom, and I run the Southern Shore. What brings you here?"

When Jacob mentioned they wanted to purchase land—and had the gold to do it—the proconsul stood. "How much can you offer?" he asked.

"Plenty." The guard deposited Jacob's backpack on the desk and unzipped the main compartment, enough to allow the proconsul to glimpse the coins inside.

"I have more, too," Jacob said. "I didn't bring it all with us."

After a moment, Proconsul Edom said, "I think we can work something out. It turns out we do have a plot of land that is currently for sale."

"Within the gates?"

"Yes. Within the gates."

"That's ... that's wonderful," Jacob stuttered.

The proconsul's lip ticked upward in a half-smile. "Martha?" he called. "Bring our guests some tea. Our very best."

Leia let herself sigh. It had been so very long since she had a good cup of tea.

Four

Southern Shore, A.D. 2042

A deep cold awakened her.

Even before Leia opened her eyes, the world spun as if it were wobbling off its axis, like a top ready to fall. She was sprawled on the forest floor, her coat gone, her pockets empty.

The red pen, missing.

She sat up and immediately regretted it. Blinking, she glanced around and tried to swallow. Jacob was nowhere in sight.

"Jacob?" she called hoarsely into the wood. "Jacob?"

She patted her right sock just above her ankle where she had hidden the single paper she had left.

It was still there.

New York City, A.D. 2027

The man tries to keep himself calm as he negotiates with the bank on how best to solve the problem of his missing life savings. "I don't understand," he repeats.

On the other end of the line, the customer service agent sighs. "Everything was transferred to another account. For privacy reasons, I cannot—"

"Privacy reasons? *Privacy reasons?* You can't be serious. Someone stole my entire—"

"Sir, I cannot disclose any information about the other account. Certainly, you understand why I cannot—"

"I understand *nothing*. Someone has transferred every single penny out of every single one of my accounts. My credit cards have been maxed out with cash advances. My money market is *gone*. My 401K—gone. My entire portfolio—gone. You need to *do* something."

"I can report the issue. Someone will contact you within five to seven business days to take your statement."

"Five to seven business days? What am I supposed to do?"

"In the meantime, I suggest filing a report with the local police department."

Five

Southern Shore, A.D. 2042

As the world began to right itself, Leia debated the merits of going back to the site where the rest of their money was hidden. Would it be wise to return to the place where Jacob had buried the rest of their gold? They hadn't talked about contingencies should one of them go missing. But the more she thought about it, the more she was convinced that he'd be waiting for her there. She was sure of it.

Leia stumbled through the forest, numb with cold, unwilling to think about what would happen if she didn't find him.

Eventually, she found the marker they'd left for themselves and there—*there!*—next to a newly dug, empty hole, lay her husband, unmoving.

She ran.

New York City, A.D. 2027

Based on the failure of his last phone call, the man thinks it would be best to report his stolen money to the precinct in person. Surely, someone will listen to him there. Someone will believe there has been an error, and help.

He tells his story to the first available policeman. A detective, he hopes. The officer listens politely.

"Yes, sir, I contacted the bank," the man says.

The officer nods. Apparently, it is the response he is looking for, and now he can file a report.

"Your name?"

The man thinks the police officer looks bored, even more than the clerk that told him his card was declined.

"Isaac Rubin."

"Address?"

In the lobby behind the man, several policemen argue with a vagrant who had barged into the precinct's front door. Before the man can respond with his address, the commotion in the lobby erupts into panic. Three officers try to tackle the newcomer. Desk legs scrape and chairs topple, as the men struggle to keep the vagrant on the floor.

"Everybody, down! He's got a gun!"

I shouldn't be here, the man thinks suddenly.

A single bullet, not intended for the man, hits him in the back.

Southern Shore, A.D. 2042

Although Jacob was covered in blood, he opened his eyes at the sound of Leia's approach.

"Jacob! Oh, God. I thought they killed you," she said, dropping down beside him, terror giving way to relief.

He shook his head, wincing. "They made me show them where we'd buried the rest of it. They told me if I didn't tell them where it was, they'd kill you. It's all gone. They took it. Everything."

"It's okay. You're here. And you'll be okay."

Her husband paused, his focus suddenly elsewhere.

"Jacob, what is it? What's wrong?"

"I don't know. I don't feel well."

She put her hand against his chest. It felt light. Airy. Strange.

No longer solid.

"Jacob?"

She frowned. Somehow, in the afternoon light, Leia could see through her husband to the dirt and leaves pressed underneath his body. He appeared soft as mist and air, growing lighter and lighter as if he was fading into memory.

His lips formed her name, but he made no sound.

Within the span of a breath, there was...nothing left.

Her hand fell through the space where her husband lay a moment before.

"Jacob!"

The sunlight hit the forest floor. Jacob was gone.

Epilogue

Upstate New York, A.D. 2049

Leia trudged up the path toward the house, shards of the bucket's plastic handle twisting into her palm. Keeping her head bowed against the stale wind not only kept her warmer, it also kept her from glancing up.

She could remember the barren hillside beneath her feet was once lush with wildflowers and promise when she had lived here with Jacob two decades before. Now, it was as if color had yielded in the same way distant armies had, pledging itself—subjugating itself—to gray, matching the sky.

Past the tree at the crest of the hill, her garden trembled in the sour air. She set the water bucket down gingerly on top of the weeds on the side of the dirt path. Jacob had used the last of the duct tape long before they left for the City, and if the plastic cracked from wear, there would be no way to fix it. No replacement.

She pried open the gate that had been cobbled together from the remains of the house down the street and stepped inside. A lifetime ago, the breeze would have smelled of rich loam and herbs, gently torn by her gardener's hand and clinging to her skin as she rid the space of weeds. Now, most of the stunted plants *were* weeds.

The plants hung limply, forlornly, their fruit small and misshapen. She reached for the tiny tomato that would be her breakfast. In the past, Leia would not even have harvested something so small. Now, the thought of casually discarding something that might mean nourishment revolted her. How spoiled she had been, how they had all been. How ungrateful.

She eased herself to the ground to begin scraping the dry earth to make a hole for the next plant she'd nurtured from seed, hoping the hard frost was past.

The tip of her finger hit something hard and long. She outlined the shape just beneath the dirt—thinner than a finger, longer than a hand.

She brushed the debris away.

There, encased in the lifeless soil, lay a pen. A *red* pen, from long years ago.

A gift—and the one thing she needed to change everything.

New York City, A.D. 2027

In the dark basement of 462 1st Avenue, the workers are gone for the day.

Hoses are curled up and hung meticulously; gurneys are clean and parked along the appropriate wall; metal surfaces are scrubbed spotless. Earlier, a woman had come and gone, numb with shock at the sudden loss of her husband from a gunshot wound, received, astonishingly, while he had been in one of the safest places in the city: a police station.

Square metal doors line one wall of the echoey room, each securely latched and sealed against the room's temperature, whether or not the contents inside require it.

Halfway up on the wall of cold stainless steel doors, a faint knocking begins.

LOST IN FORM
Rachel Sharpton

"There, that's the turnoff."

He squinted, slowing down to make sure he could see the diverging branch of asphalt between the tall hedgerows that lined the dual carriageway. The car sputtered as it downshifted into lower gear, and he cursed under his breath, fearing yet another engine stall.

"All good over there?"

He could feel the judging stare from his travelling companion as though it were the midday sun. Their condescending tone was not lost on him either, but he tried to pay it no mind. Over the course of their travels, he had come to learn that Asra was only baiting him with this kind of talk. After more than a few years in these forms, they still had not found the healthiest of ways to pass the time travelling in meatspace.

Asra was simply bored. It would pass.

Gritting his teeth, he made the turn slowly while keeping a white-knuckled hand on the gear shift. An even smaller road winded out in front of them, and he leaned forward over the steering wheel, trying to anticipate whether any oncoming cars would be barrelling around the corners—an all too familiar experience in these back roads of the Welsh countryside.

"Are you sure this is the right way?" he said, trying to keep his eyes on the road while also taking in his surroundings, which were, as expected, quite green and arboreal.

Asra scoffed, as he knew they would. It was like being on stage, starring in roles that they were born to play. He and Asra didn't need to think about it anymore. Their morning ritual of practising gestures, tone of voice, and inflection had long since been phased out. They were becoming native. Much more quickly than perhaps they both realised.

"Of course, it is. Have I ever led you astray?"

"Do you really want to go there with me right now?"

"Okay, fine. Have I led you astray in the last year?"

He carefully made another turn around a sharp bend, sighing in relief when he saw the road straighten out before them.

"No," he admitted. "You're improving."

"Wish I could say the same about your driving."

"Manual was the only option they had. Be quiet or take up the wheel yoursel—"

"There!" Asra interrupted, pointing ahead and off to the side. "Look."

A road sign: Hay-on-Wye, 3m.

"See?" Asra folded their arms, a smug grin twitching at the corners of their mouth. "I told you. I read the map correctly."

"Fine," he conceded. "Let's just hope your hunch is right. We *need* a power source. Badly. I haven't been able to broadcast anything for a week. It's getting exhausting using only words to talk to you."

"Why do you think I brought music along, Lloyd? I'm also getting tired of your voice. I don't know if I'll ever get used to it in this form, to be honest."

"Oh, yes. Great music selection we have here." He flipped up the centre divider and fumbled around inside with one hand, feeling for the distinct hard plastic edges of a CD case. "All of two choices," he said, tossing them onto Asra's lap. "The greatest hits of David Bowie and the Phantom of the Opera original broadcast recording. Surely, these won't become grating after days on the road."

"What are you talking about? David Bowie is all we need."

"Well, all *I* need is silence. And maybe a vanilla soft serve cone with a smattering of sprinkles on top. Anyway, it doesn't matter. We're here. The book town. Finally."

He pulled off the road into a small car park, just outside the town limits. Stepping out of the car, he checked his watch.

"It's only nine thirty," he said as he opened the boot. "We're too early to check in. Are any of the bookshops open?"

Asra groaned as they stretched. With a wide yawn, they shook out their long dark hair before twisting it up into a messy bun. "Maybe? At the very least, we could grab a bite to eat first. I'm starving."

"Sure. But what can we expect for food in a town filled with bookstores?"

He glanced at Asra, who shot him a familiar, shit eating grin. "Knowledge."

It took everything within his power to hold back an exasperated sigh, but he vowed not to grant Asra such a thrill.

"Right."

Without another word, he closed and locked the boot, then dug his hands into his jean pockets, kicking a few stones as he trudged forward into town.

***

Under normal circumstances, Lloyd would be charmed by a town like this. It was one that, even in this age, seemed rare to stumble upon. The brown stone buildings were typical of this region, but what was unusual were the rows upon rows of bookstores lining the small streets. Hay-on-Wye sat right on the border of England and Wales and had developed a reputation over time for being a haven of used bookstores. Big box chain stores across the country catered to the masses, while the vendors of Hay-on-Wye catered to those who were looking for that diamond in the rough. Something that they could boast about finding upon returning to their big city lives.

This reputation for limited and rare selections was what caught Lloyd and Asra's attention in the first place. It had been weeks since they had been able to access and make use of a powerful enough energy source. They hoped some answers would lie here. But searching for a diamond amidst the rubble wouldn't be easy. Yet even as Lloyd and Asra wandered around the city, they felt a change in the energy around them: a stirring in the air akin to the moments before a lightning strike.

Whatever it was seemed to grow in strength the further they went into town. The energy ebbed and flowed, like the coming and going of high and low tide, and they were unconsciously drawn towards it, like moths to a flame. Both surprised and perhaps a touch overwhelmed, the two travelers quickly found a cafe where they could wordlessly discuss these findings over a couple of stuffed jacket potatoes.

Stars, this feels amazing. A weight off my shoulders.

Yes, but the signal is patchy. We need to find the source. I have to strain to broadcast more than a few words.

Like squeezing extra hard on a poo.

Lloyd dropped his fork and glared at Asra, pushing his plate away. "Really?"

Asra, as though almost expecting this outrage, immediately swiped the half-eaten dish from Lloyd and dug into it. "We'll have to go store by store to better gauge where it might be coming from," they said in between bites.

Lloyd groaned. "That's going to take ages."

"Yeah well," Asra said, stifling a burp. "We could try to just lean into the energy's signature to find the source, but that hasn't worked out too well for us recently, has it?"

Asra shot him a pointed look, and Lloyd cringed, recalling a very specific example. It used to be so much easier. Like breathing. Everything was back then—when they first arrived on the planet's surface. But that was so long ago.

Lloyd exhaled a resigned sigh and then signaled to their server to deliver the bill. "Then let's get started, shall we? I don't want to have to extend the booking."

Asra nodded, their eyes shining with resolve, even as Lloyd still saw a flicker of doubt cross over their features. When the bill arrived, Lloyd set a twenty-pound note on top of it and told the server to keep the change.

"Oh, miss," Asra said as the server was about to leave. "I was just curious—do you happen to know which stores here might specialise in books about the obscure, weird, and unusual?"

She shook her head. "Can't say I do. Sorry, loves. But you should ask Greg. He runs the Old Black Lion. He knows everything about this town."

"Wonderful. That happens to be exactly where we're staying. Thank you so much, Amelia. You have a great day, now."

***

Asra stood next to Lloyd, hands on their hips, looking up at the shop's blade sign that dangled above them: *Cat's Cradle: Chronicles and Curiosities*. Lloyd glanced at the operating hours listed on the glass door. *Weekdays: 10:00 – 17:00.*

"We better hurry," he said. "We only have about an hour left."

Asra balked. "Stars. Were we really talking to Greg for that long?"

"Not many tourists this time of year, clearly." Lloyd rolled his neck to stretch it. The days spent driving around the island nation had taken their toll. "Well, this is the only other shop Greg told us about, so we can always come back tomorrow."

"Nah, fuck it. We're here. Let's do this."

The familiar chime of a shop bell greeted them as they passed through the threshold. In response, a hoarse, yet upbeat voice called out to them from the back. The shopkeeper, no doubt.

"Alrighi, just a moment please."

"Oh, no rush," Asra replied. "We'll just have a look around."

The first thing they noticed inside was the smell: sickly sweet with a heavy musk that assaulted the senses. It smelled like the incense someone would burn with the intention of camouflaging the weighty stench of cigarette smoke. Lloyd wrinkled his nose in response, his eyes watering, and attempted to stifle a sneeze. Failing to do so, he quickly tucked his nose into the crook of his arm to muffle most of the sound.

"Bless you," Asra whispered, handing him a fresh tissue.

Lloyd nodded in thanks and then blew his nose. "Ugh. What do you think he's trying to cover up with that?" He spoke softly, in case the shopkeeper might be listening.

"I don't know. But it's not bothering me as much as you, clearly. I think it's kind of homey. Like stepping into the house of a distant relative who keeps a jar of decade-old candy on the coffee table just in case you might want one."

Lloyd raised an eyebrow in amusement. "That was an oddly specific observation."

"Yes, well, humans often are."

All traces of mirth left his face in an instant, and he scrunched up his nose again as a reflex response, either to stifle another sneeze or to express disgust at being reminded that he had been wearing this form for far too long already. Looking around, Lloyd actually wasn't sure if it was the incense or the layer of dust on nearly everything above arm's reach that had caused him to sneeze. Between that and the piles of unorganised books that sat stacked on nearly every free surface, it was hard to tell if the shopkeeper had just moved in, was planning to move out, or just simply existed like this.

He shifted his weight, rubbing at the back of his neck. "Maybe Greg was wrong about this place."

Asra turned to him, surprised. "Don't be ridiculous. I think this is exactly the kind of place we're looking for."

"Do you, now?" said the hoarse voice from the back as the shopkeeper came into view. "Well, I'm chuffed to hear that."

He came lumbering towards them—a giant of a man with the posture of someone who spent most of their waking hours slumped over volumes of text. It was the first good sign since entering the shop and meant that he probably knew his inventory well. Lloyd had not seen any kind of computer inventory system. He was likely to be running things more old-school.

"Welcome," he continued, before being stopped by a quick succession of sharp coughs, as though the short walk had winded him. "You boys hail from America or Canada? I never assume anymore. Not since the last Canadians I mistook for Americans never let me hear the end of it."

"America," Asra said, taking the lead in the conversation, per usual. "Though not by choice."

This earned them a hearty guffaw from the shopkeeper, and the deep reverberation of his laughter seemed to immediately clear the space, like a sunbeam cutting through a cluster of dense clouds. In this lightness, Lloyd could sense something else, though it was only for a fleeting moment. It felt like the buzz of static electricity, raising the hair on his arms. And underneath each thunderclap of laughter, he could hear a low, monotonous droning.

As soon as he was aware of it, an image flashed in the back of his mind: an echo of a memory, from a time long past, when friends gathered together and watched nebulas give birth to star clusters. They had marveled at the sight, knowing that this promised them endless worlds to discover. Endless adventures to be had. For the first time in a long time, Lloyd saw his true self, somehow, in the spaces between a stranger's laughter.

He stumbled backwards, his balance off-center, as though he had suddenly forgotten how to function in this body. Steadying himself, he shot Asra a quick glance. They were already looking at him, wide-eyed and alert, as though they had experienced the exact same vision and sensation.

Was that—

An energy shift, yes.

From him, or ...?

Maybe. Discuss later.

Thankfully, the shopkeeper didn't seem to pick up on their confused reactions, or if he did, he had no intention of commenting on it, continuing instead with his congenial sales pitch.

"So, what can I do you for? I got some Dickens, as you might expect, but I take it that's not why you stumbled into my shop. Did Greg refer you?"

"Yes," Lloyd said, clearing his throat, his mind still reeling from the potent energy shift. "We're on the hunt for something a bit more esoteric, you might say."

"Then you've come to the right place," the shopkeeper said, the tone of his voice now rich and inviting.

"Excellent," Asra said, their voice a touch shaky. Strangers wouldn't have been able to pick up on it. But Lloyd could. "We're collectors, you understand. Of the weird and obscure. Especially when it comes to local legends."

The shopkeeper only nodded knowingly as he turned around and lumbered towards the back of the store, running his fingers along the spines of the books along the way, as though greeting old friends. "You researching something for a book of your own?"

"Something like that," Asra said, purposefully vague. "It's just a special interest. You know, some people are into trainspotting. Others collect stamps. We're interested in legends. Myths. Stretching the limits of human imagination."

He clicked his tongue. "You know, folk used to think differently about that kind stuff. Was more than just stories for them. Well, I 'spose they were hurtin' for entertainment and the like." He stopped to look up and down a small section in the corner. "Can you be a bit more specific, lads? I've also got stock in the back that could suit ya."

"These will do for now," Asra said hurriedly. "We know you're closing soon."

The shopkeeper nodded, then shuffled over to a door that had a *Staff Only* sign taped precariously above it. "Tidy. Don't worry—take your time. I'll let you know when I'm about to lock up. Ta."

Lloyd caught a good glimpse of what lay beyond the door as the shopkeeper opened it. Amongst the additional piles of unorganised mess, something caught his attention: a thick, red, leather-bound book with faded gold-embossed lettering on the spine and smouldering edges, as though it had been saved last minute from a burning building. The energy emanating out of it was palpable, and once he fixed his eyes upon it, he could not look away.

Suddenly, a sharp pain shot through his temple, and a flurry of images whirred past his consciousness, as though he was getting a sudden download of information all at once. It overwhelmed him. But there was no mistaking it, now. This was what had caused the energy shift just moments ago, and what had given him temporary access to his true self. This glimpse of what he once was—all triggered by this unexpectedly curious book—was like being given a miniscule dose of a tantalizing substance. He desperately wanted more. Before he could stop himself, he pointed out the book excitedly.

"Hang on. What's that one back there?"

The shopkeeper looked behind to where he was pointing.

"Oh," he said. His tone sounded like he was trying to remain indifferent. "That one? I'm not sure, but I do have some of my own personal collection stashed back there. Some not for sale."

"I see," Lloyd said, his attention still fixated on the forbidden book.

The shopkeeper shifted his weight, as though deciding how to proceed. He looked at both of them, then back at the book that Lloyd had so eagerly pointed out. After a considerable pause, his features relaxed into a warm smile.

"Tell you what. Since you boys came all the way from America," he paused, digging into one of the lined inner pockets of his jacket before producing a small, engraved stainless steel cigarette case. "I'd like to try to help you fill up that collection of yours."

He opened the case and handed them both a business card on thick card stock, which probably had been eggshell white at some point. Lloyd looked down at the yellowing card and the block lettering.

RHYS EVANS, PROPRIETOR

CAT'S CRADLE: CHRONICLES AND CURIOSITIES

8 BEAR STREET

"A few of us owners in town get together at the Lion to discuss new findings and exchange business advice," Rhys continued. "Next one is this Saturday night. I figure more heads are better than one, especially one as dingy as mine. Why don't you give me a call by four tomorrow and I'll let you know the details? You don't have any other plans, do you?"

***

The sunset was quite spectacular that Saturday evening. They had just caught the tail end of it, having spent most of the day buried in the volumes they had accumulated from their shopping spree the last couple of days. Lloyd glanced at the clock on the wall then back down at his watch, comparing the two times. He narrowed his eyes when he realised that they were a couple minutes out of sync, and he did not know which one displayed the correct time.

"Hello? Void? Anyone home? Did you hear what I said?" Asra tossed a satsuma in his direction, but just missed him, hitting the box of tissues on the table instead.

Lloyd frowned. "Don't use that name here. What if you slip up, like you did in Texas?"

Asra shot him a murderous glare, one that would have withered him when they first arrived on the planet, as they were still both unfamiliar in their chosen forms. Now, deadly looks like these were a common occurrence. Perhaps he had just gotten used to daily discomfort.

"Don't patronise me," Asra snapped. "It's your name, isn't it? What have you done in the last hour, anyway? You've lost your edge ever since we went into that damn shop. It's like pulling teeth with you, I swear."

Lloyd reached down for the satsuma and smoothed his thumb over it. Squeezing it slightly, he gave it a sniff. It was still not ripe enough to eat. Standing up, he tossed the satsuma back and forth in his hands, walking over to the mantle above the defunct fireplace in their twin-bedded room. In its place, an arrangement of gnarled, stick-like artificial greenery sat in an oversized vase that still bore the price tag from the charity shop from where it had been procured.

Lining the mantle was an assortment of trinkets with no unifying theme. When they had first checked in, Asra surmised they were probably left behind by former guests who must have come to the conclusion that they were not worth the postage it would have cost to return them. He set the satsuma down next to a plaid pincushion monogrammed with the initials "D.T." in green thread. Next to that was a ball bearing pendulum. He picked up one of the balls at the end and let it go, taking a small step back to watch the pendulum in action, the ball's momentum creating a pleasing tapping rhythm.

"Asra," he said, his tone becoming soft. "What do you think happened to Envoy?"

Silence followed. There was only the tapping of the pendulum undercut with the sound of Asra sucking in a deep, shuddering breath.

"Envoy," Asra said reluctantly, as though even just saying the name caused them tremendous sadness. The heaviness of it seemed to fill the room and darken it. "Stars, it's been ages since I even thought of them."

"Isn't that strange? And to think they were supposed to accompany us here. Yet, like you, I haven't thought of them much at all. Until now."

He turned to look at Asra, who had their eyes cast down, an open book on their lap.

"I did at first," they said, their voice barely audible. "Often, in fact. I hoped, at least, that they might break out somehow and join us. Now, after everything, I'm not sure who has been met with a worse fate."

Lloyd turned back around, focusing all his attention on the swinging pendulum. "I was reminded of them in the shop, when we interacted with Rhys. That shift in energy. It felt so familiar and sparked a moment of cosmic clarity for me. Like being splashed with cold water on a winter morning."

Asra looked up, their dark eyes reflecting the harsh light of the fluorescent bulb overhead. "You don't think he's ... one of *us*, do you? I mean, how could that be?"

"I don't know. But lately, all we're doing here just seems to be delaying the inevitable. I can feel myself slipping away, Asra." He clenched his fists. "And I hate it. I hate it so much."

By this time, the pendulum's swing had dwindled down to more of a laborious plonking than a satisfied tapping, so Lloyd stuck his hand in to stop the momentum all at once. Asra opened their mouth, then closed it again, remaining silent.

"I don't want to end up like one of these," he gestured to the trinkets on the mantle. "Lost in form. Just another forgotten memento from someone's holiday."

It had become so still in their room that he could feel his heartbeat thumping against his eardrums. Finally, Asra broke the tension by shifting their weight on the bed. Their broadcast followed shortly after.

Don't think that I have forgiven myself, Void. After all these years. The guilt weighs on me like an anvil.

I know. But I've told you over and over that it's not all your fault. I wasn't forced into coming here. Neither was Envoy. We both chose this.

No. None of us chose to be trapped. None of us chose to slowly forget who we are.

If you knew that was going to happen, you never would have suggested coming here. Grieve if you must, but the guilt will kill you before these forms do.

You're right that we have to do something. But that book in Rhys's shop? Taking it will be yet another low vibrational act, pulling us further down towards the abyss.

I know. But what choice do we have?

***

The lock on the backdoor of the shop was so easy to pick, it may as well have not been locked at all. He realized that it was merely a gesture. Clearly, Rhys did not ever expect to be robbed. Though he tried to push it out of his mind, he could feel the guilt drip in slowly, as though being filtered through a fine sieve.

"We get in and get out quick," he whispered. Remember, we're only here for the book."

Though it was too dark to see clearly, he knew he was getting another one of Asra's signature deadly glares. "This wasn't my idea, you know," they hissed.

Once inside, the pull of the book was immediate. No lights were necessary to find its location. The energy lured them both there like fish to bait, and when they reached the table where it sat, Lloyd's hands trembled as he hovered them over it.

"Well," Asra said, sounding rather drained despite being near the energy source. "There it is. You'll do the honors, I suppose?"

Lloyd only nodded. Carefully, he lifted up the book's hefty front cover. As he did so, a small gleam of light appeared from within the center, growing brighter the wider the book was opened. They both gasped when they realized what they were looking at. In place of pages of text, there was a hollowed-out center holding a small object, blacker than the purest obsidian. The glow emanating from it changed from a soft blue light to a dark maroon. Small, intricate carvings ran up and down its oval shape, and Lloyd thought they were just decorative flourishes before he reached his hand out to pick it up.

As soon as he did, he was struck with a vision, stronger than anything he had experienced since arriving on this cosmos-forsaken, remote-ass rock. It overtook him completely, but he could see and feel that Asra had been pulled into it as well, even though Asra had not yet touched the object. A myriad of scenes flickered at breakneck speed—visual records from the presumed owner of the object. Cascading skylines and dripping sunsets on a planet with violet-tinted skies in a galaxy that looked familiar, but yet somehow very foreign. Lush foliage and sweeping vistas greeted them from every angle, as though they were looking out from the point of view of every sentient being on the planet's surface.

Then, everything suddenly collapsed, like the impossibly heavy center of a dying star, pulling all matter and energy towards a black, endless void, until all at once, everything went white, and they were met with a person looking at their reflection in a mirror. A human male. Familiar eyes, not as old. Hair full and lush, with not a speck of grey to be seen. A tall man, with an easy smile and broad shoulders—ones that were not yet bent forward by the weight of time. He winked at the reflection, then shifted into his true, formless self before reverting back to his human shape as though nothing had happened.

It was Rhys. A much younger Rhys. When he still knew who he truly was. Before he was lost in form.

The vision stopped, and Lloyd dropped the object as though he had just been handling hot coals. He gasped for breath, with Asra following suit. It was as though they had been held under water, unable to breathe during the entire experience. Asra coughed and leaned forward, gripping the ends of the desk as though to steady themselves.

Fuck. You were right. He was ... no, he is—

Like us. Rhys is trapped here, just like us.

Lloyd heard Asra sniff. They were crying.

I can't do it, Void. I was already reluctant to just take this, but now... we can't just leave him here. Can we? If he's here, then there might be others.

Lloyd straightened his back, the dripping of guilt turning into a loud, leaky faucet. He was unable to push it back any longer.

Then, it seems, our primary directive has changed.

He closed the book solemnly, shutting out the last bit of light that pulsated out from the object. He shuddered, as though he had somehow closed a door that he would never be able to open again. To his surprise, he felt Asra's hand smooth over his upper back, a feeling of immense warmth emanating out from them.

There's still time. We can find them and help them remember. Somehow. We'll find a way. I know it. We've been through worse together, Void.

For once, Lloyd did not balk at the use of his true name. The corners of his mouth twitched into a half smile, before he exhaled a shaky breath and cleared his throat.

"What are you waiting for, then? It's eight thirty. If we go now, Rhys and the others will probably be there. We still have time, don't we?"

NAMING MY DEMON

Rosalie A. Peng

My husband was silent as he listened. His smile faded, and the sharp crescents of his nails dug into the skin of my belly.

"What is it?" I asked. I tried to push him off, eager to relieve my bladder. But he refused to budge. His ear was glued to my distended abdomen, and his brows were furrowed like he was detangling a logic game.

"Can you hear them?" he finally asked.

"What are you talking about?" I shoved him off and rubbed my stomach. "I can feel them, though. Baby A is a kicker, and Baby B will give Simone Biles a run for her money." The strangeness of his question hit me. The new moms who returned to my pregnancy support group had shared the most bonkers things their husbands said in the delivery room, but this was four months premature. "What do you mean by 'hear them'?"

"It's nothing, sweetheart," he said a bit too quickly. He must've seen that flicker of anxiety on my face. After two miscarriages that quaked our marriage and my recent preeclampsia diagnosis, my burnt-out nerves stood rigid like the ends of fried hair as we inched into the last trimester. It didn't take much to send me spiraling into dark ruminations.

It's nothing, sweetheart. That was easy for him to say, but the troubling thoughts didn't go away. Pregnancy could be a one-way ticket across the rainbow to a land of sunshine, carpools, and the joys of motherhood—if you were lucky. But if you were like me, whose treacherous womb managed to convert every *what-if* into somber reality, pregnancy was a deep, stygian pit that filled my mind with too many worries and unknowns to name.

Those unknowns were the scariest. Things are scarier when you can't name them. I learned this when my therapist finally slapped the OCD label on my intrusive thoughts and immobilizing anxiety, shining a rational light on them. Out of the darkness, they were suddenly easier to bear. Psychologically, knowing a *what-if's* name makes it less intimidating and threatening. My therapist explained it this way: "It's kind of like how an exorcist bellows the demon's name in horror movies and, in the name of the Lord, banishes him to the pits of hell."

She told me that naming my demons gave me power over them. I knew some of their names already. *Morning sickness. Gestational diabetes. Preeclampsia. Miscarriage. Postpartum depression. Prolapse. Stillbirth—*

STOP.

If I went down this rabbit hole, eventually, I'd encounter those nameless *what-ifs.* My therapist would be disappointed. My husband would be annoyed. And I'd be terrified.

So instead, I distracted myself by putting together the nursery. The twin cribs were made of iron, set with soft blankets, and shielded by canopies of muslin and lace. I sat fluffy teddy bears and delicate porcelain dolls on shelves above both cribs; rocking horses and dollhouses awaited at their sides. Blankets, onesies, and itty-bitty little shoes filled the twin drawers. I hung the glow-in-the-dark stars in their skies, delighted at how the vinyl fluoresced when I flicked off the lights.

When the day's work was done, I lay next to my husband, tossing and turning until I found a comfortable position. The clock struck midnight, and I awoke. There was a rustling noise, like leaves scraping on the sidewalk as the wind pulled them into flight. *Did we leave a window open?* A quick look at the window answered in the negative.

Then I heard it—and *felt* it. My heartbeat skidded to a halt. Cold sweat oozed from my pores as small, disembodied voices haunted my ears. *Where were they coming from?* They sounded close, uncomfortably close. For a moment, I thought I had finally lost my mind and had started hearing voices in my head. But the voices spoke again, and shuddering with misplaced relief, I realized they originated from much lower in my body. It was different from how my voice vibrated in that spot between my breasts; these little quakes came from my abdomen, and my stomach tumbled each time the sounds rang. I rubbed my belly . Muffled gurgles rumbled in the night as though the speakers were trapped underwater.

Or, I realized, trapped in a sack of fluid.

"Stop kicking me! Your foot's in my face!"

"Not my fault you're fat. I don't have enough room!"

The skin of my belly rippled. My hand jumped away like my belly was some dirty thing. *What's in there?* My mind swam through catalogs of alien creatures that could be chirping away inside my womb. Shivers weaved through my vertebrae, and my skin erupted in gooseflesh. But then the voices were gone, silenced like an interrupted dream. *I must've dreamt it,* I decided as sleepy grogginess rolled over my mind like a fog descending over a quiet lake. It cloaked everything in a sheen of surrealism and numbed my fear and revulsion for the lump on my abdomen. I felt a dopey smile tug at my lips—what was there to be afraid of? These were my girls, my babies.

"Honey, I hear them," I muttered as I fell asleep. When the sun rose, I thought no more of those tiny bickers I heard, sure they were the stuff of dreams and nightmares.

***

Two months later, I held Mina in my arms. But her sister Lucy went the way of her tragic namesake. My husband and I had met at a college book club, and we decided to name our girls after our favorite book's leading ladies. But it wasn't Count Dracula who took Lucy from me; it was her umbilical cord. During birth, it became her noose. I had hanged my daughter.

My husband and I grieved as we fed and changed Mina, then grieved some more during those hours when she slept. I cried myself to sleep the first night postpartum and cried myself awake just past the witching hour. Rinse and repeat.

A month after the birth, when I could no longer stand looking at that pink nursery with its two cribs, two sets of teddy bears, porcelain dolls, blankets, little shoes, and rocking horses, we took down the spares. I gave the crib and horse to a neighbor and wept as I tucked the rest into a large chest for storage in the attic.

One night, I jolted awake before the tear tracks on my cheeks had dried. I squinted into the dark corners of the room, confused by my disquiet. Then I heard it—the sound that had jolted me from restless slumber. It sounded different—it had lost that warped, submerged quality—but I knew it was the same voice: *my daughter's voice!*

My hand leaped to my empty stomach. I gripped the loose skin, searching for my lost child in vain. Her weight wasn't there, nor were the vibrations that filled my abdomen when she spoke. I bit back my disappointment, which threatened to escape as a sob. The baby monitor crackled on the nightstand, and Mina's shrill cries barged into our room. I dabbed my eyes before my husband could see my tears and shushed him back to sleep.

"I'll take care of her," I said. I wanted to hold my baby.

One night, I heard the voice—*Lucy's voice*—again. I sat up, gasping. On cue, I patted my stomach, feeling for her, but felt no vibrations. Throwing my pillow over my snoring husband's face, I listened hard in the night. Disembodied whispers crackled over the staticky baby monitor. I sprang out of bed and grabbed the speaker, my footsteps gentle as I crept down the dark hallway toward the nursery. Sounds spilled from the monitor. I clamped my lips into a stiff line as though sewn together by a mortician, refusing to set the bubbling scream free.

"It's cold out here. I miss Mother's womb. Mother's womb was warm."

Outside the amniotic sac, the girlish voice was high and crisp, as light as a cloud.

"Stop complaining, Mina," said her twin. Her voice had a breathy translucence to it, misting about like a dancing phantom. *"You have it better. Your flesh keeps you warm. I'm so cold, I'll freeze to death!"*

The nursery door was ajar. I crammed my fingers into my mouth to stifle my screams. Darkness swarmed behind the crib's canopy. Two infants' silhouettes were black against the muslin and lace. They sat on their pudgy bottoms like teddy bears, facing each other in the crib as they conversed. Lucy's name fluttered through my mind as saliva-slicked fingers dropped from my mouth. Fear locked my body, but desperation for my child—to *hold her*, to *know her*—pushed me into the room. I approached quietly as the baby monitor croaked garbled static that droned on and on.

I flicked on the lights. I ran to the crib and whipped open the canopy. Mina lay flat on her back, looking at me with big eyes. Her blankets were askew, and despite knowing better, I yanked them away in case they hid another infant. My breaths became choking sobs as I tore apart the room, opening closets and pulling out drawers, searching for another child.

At last, I leaned my head against the dresser and sank to my knees. There was no other child. Giving one last sob, I wiped my eyes and steadied my breaths. *Pull yourself together*, I chastised. My therapist had named my most recent demon: postpartum depression. Coaxing it back to hell would take more than a few sprinkles of holy water and Hail Marys. *But now, I knew its name!* So, it could be done—and *must* be done soon—since my husband was already walking on eggshells around me. I didn't need him or my therapist questioning my sanity.

Wiping my eyes, I tucked Mina into the blankets. "Are you cold, sweetie?" I whispered. I swallowed before speaking again. "If you're cold, Mommy will bring you another blanket."

Her eyes glittered with an old intelligence that *shouldn't* belong to a child. For a second, I feared she'd answer. That she'd reveal herself to be some new *what-if* that had no name. But she said nothing. She was still my baby.

***

My husband was short-tempered on a good day, and good days came fewer and fewer as Mina learned to talk, talk back, and then swear. She was a wild child: loud, disruptive, sometimes downright nasty. In preschool, she pushed other kids on the playground and tore up their artwork; in the first grade, she threw rocks at passing kids on bikes and yanked the neighbor's cat's tail. Her vocabulary was as colorful as her raging temper was frightening. She was only docile during those odd hours at night when I'd catch her whispering into the dark.

I was doing the dishes when my husband's roar echoed through the house, followed by Mina's enraged shriek. The plate in my hand slipped and crashed as shouting erupted from the attic. I hurried upstairs.

I suppressed a wail at what I saw. The large chest was opened, its contents scattered in pieces on the musty, cobwebbed floor. Hurricane Mina had swept through the attic, leaving none of her deceased sister's keepsakes untouched. Tears welled in my eyes as I saw Lucy's decapitated teddy bear, bleeding white fluff from the stump of its neck. The bear's head was nowhere to be found. The porcelain doll's curly ringlets and chiffon dress had been torn off, and its limbs ripped from the hallowed torso. Mina had tossed the blankets and unworn baby shoes carelessly onto the ground.

"What the hell is wrong with you?" my husband screamed. His opened hand landed—*wham! wham! wham!*—on Mina's buttocks. "Look at me!" He grabbed her face. Anger flushed Mina's face, and she ignored my husband as she hissed angry nonsense, staring into the dark corners of the attic. She clutched her old baby monitor in her hands.

My husband's eyes flashed as he knocked the monitor from Mina's hands and shoved her away. "I'm going on a drive!" he yelled, but what I heard was: *I'm leaving.*

Years ago, during my pregnancy, I would've tolerated his outbursts—I would've begged and pleaded for him to stay as I had after each miscarriage. But now, I was furious. Mina ignited fires wherever she went, and I was too tired to keep putting them out while also keeping my husband's tantrums at bay. I no longer dreaded—no, *feared*—his rage. All I felt was anger. How *dare* he lay a hand on my child? Scouring every last wrinkle on his face, I couldn't find a trace of the man I married. I wanted this tyrant out.

"Leave, then!" I screeched, speeding to my daughter's side.

"Oh, I will," he growled. "You deal with this demon you birthed!"

Before I could retort, Mina strode up to her father, seething. The crown of her head barely reached his pelvis, but for a split second, he cowered as though she was a giant.

"Daddy," she said sweetly, "you're gonna die tonight." He sputtered, his face a disgruntled purple shade, and she continued, "Lucy told me so."

He stomped out. We listened to him slam the front door, and Mina skipped downstairs, quite unperturbed. I stared after her, too shocked and distressed to ask about her utterance. Unwilling to part with Lucy's belongings, I traipsed through the attic in a daze, tidying the wrecked toys back into the chest.

Hours later, two uniformed officers knocked on my door, their cruisers lighting up the neighborhood in red and blue. My mind was blank as they told me *there had been an accident, ma'am*, and *we're very sorry for your loss.*

It wasn't your husband's fault, the cops assured me, *the other driver swore there was a little girl out on the road. Said he had to swerve into oncoming traffic to avoid hitting her.*

The police completed their investigation. No little girl was ever found.

***

"Have you seen my dentures?" my mother asked as we worked in the garden. "I've lost them somewhere in that house of yours."

"I'll ask Mina if she took them." I sighed. "She's been squirreling things away. She's taken coat hangers from my closet and snipped the buttons off my jackets. God knows what she's up to. What if . . ."

I hesitated to verbalize the rest. But with my mother as my only audience, tales of Mina's disturbing behavior burst from my mouth in a deluge. I caught myself beginning every other sentence with those cursed words, *what if?*

"What if . . . there is something wrong—no, *evil*—about her?" I asked softly. I told my mother everything: from the whispers I heard coming from my womb, to the two silhouettes in Mina's crib, to Mina's ominous proclamation the night my husband died. "I'm a jumpy sack of nerves around her. Her eyes don't look like a kid's. I—I must be a terrible mother to think of my child like this." I blinked away tears. "I'm just so tired."

Like any mother—terrible or not—I knew my daughter. I knew her favorite color was blue. I knew she hated brussels sprouts. And of course, I knew her name. Yet there was something about her I couldn't grasp. She carried it through the house, and I flinched each time I tried to make sense of it. With that nameless thing, she brought my *what-ifs* to life. And like an exorcist facing off against a new, unknown demonic foe, I was powerless to banish it. I feared a future with her.

My mother never believed in the supernatural. "It's all a coincidence, hun," she said. "You've had some rotten luck, that's all. Mina's a sweet child." With my husband gone, I had rejoined the workforce and often left Mina in my mother's care. She'd taken to teaching Mina how to sew during those hours. "Good with a needle, too, but feisty. Dry your eyes, dear."

I was in slightly better spirits when we strode back into the house, but upon entering the kitchen room, my mother gasped, and my heartbeat tripped erratically.

A *Thing* was sitting at my dining room table.

It was grotesque. I fought the urge to vomit as I recognized the jigsaw pieces that formed its body. It wore the porcelain doll's tattered chiffon dress and tangled blond wig. The decapitated teddy bear's head sat under the wig, its brown fur dirty and matted. The jagged edge of its neck had been neatly stitched into the doll's dress.

A gash had been ripped in the bear's head right where the mouth should be. The slash stretched across the bear's face in a too-wide grin. My mother's missing dentures were stuffed into the slit, the pink gums looking almost red next to the exposed white stuffing. The bear's eyes were mismatched buttons from my jackets. The right one was small and red; the left one was nearly triple its twin's size and pitch-black like coal. The doll's stubby legs wobbled from beneath the dress, wearing Lucy's baby shoes. The arms protruding out of the dress's ballooned sleeves were the curved hooks of the missing coat hangers. The sharp wires glistened.

I stared at The Thing and mentally named it *Frankenstein*. It looked like Victor Frankenstein's preschool project, built of stolen toys from his classmates' cubbies instead of body parts from robbed graves—a hellish effigy of an anthropomorphized stuffed bear.

"W–What the hell is that?" my mother blustered. She stomped to the table and held The Thing up to examine it. "Are these my dentures? What has that daughter of yours been doing?"

"Mina!" I screamed and scrambled into the hallway. No response. I ran back to the kitchen. "Mom! Mina's gone—"

My mother stared at me, jaw slack, blood leaking out the sides of her mouth. She clutched The Thing at chest level. The Thing's hooked arm—*no, a hanger, not an arm*—threaded through her throat like a curved needle. My mother retched twice; each time, the rounded end of the hanger bulged under her skin. Her terrified eyes met mine as she mouthed, *Help me!*

"No!" I screamed when her arm twitched, and I knew what she was about to do.

She shuddered. A spurt of life and strength shocked through her, and she tore the hanger out of her neck. Blood sprayed onto the tablecloth. Flecks of flesh followed suit, splattering onto my pristine kitchen floors as a dark red pool formed at my mother's feet. Her eyes rolled wildly, and she fell forward. I stood in shock for a full minute before regaining my senses. I screamed and ran to her. Suddenly, my eyes popped, and I tripped to the ground as her body jerked.

My mother's upper body bobbed, and two curved wire hands clawed out from underneath her bulk, dragging The Thing's now deformed body. The head tilted up to stare at me through mismatched eyes, my mother's blood staining dark streaks on the bear's fur. The stuffing between my mother's dentures eagerly soaked up her blood. The Thing stunk of mold and iron, and I retched as it wobbled towards me. From behind the stuffing came the awful, familiar sound of crackling static. Though it had been years since I used it, I recognized its grainy drawl immediately. *The baby monitor,* I realized, *is inside The Thing's body!*

"Mommy?"

Mina stood in the doorway, oddly calm, as she surveyed her grandmother's exsanguinating body. I tried to warn her, tried to tell her to run away, but fear and shock rendered me speechless. She carried a musty old baby blanket in her arms, and her bare feet pitter-pattered as she stepped around the pooling blood and picked The Thing up. To my horror, she kissed it on its bloody cheek and sat it back in its chair.

"There you go, Lucy," she smiled as she wrapped the blanket around it.

The effigy's grotesque head twitched around to face me, and I named my little demon, my daughter, my lost child: *Lucy.* The last of my consciousness drained away as her voice cracked over the baby monitor.

"It's finally warm, Mommy."

THE PECHMANS' DENOUEMENT

Jason Herrington

"Oh. My. God! This place is incredible!" Susie Pechman said, mouth agape. Her left hand clawed into her husband's thigh as she took in her surroundings. Towering evergreens interspersed with gold-leafed perennials climbed the slope outside her passenger window. The tires grumbled up the graveled drive as glimpses of the house came into view, the glassy lake stretching majestically beyond.

"Happy tenth anniversary, my love. Wait 'til you see the entire property." Elias gave Susie a sidelong glance, feeling incredibly grateful, as enamored by her beauty as the day they'd first met. As he maneuvered through the gate, the lake house came fully into view: a stylish expanse of limestone, dark wood, large windows, and sleek angles. Elias swelled with pride. He knew not many men could afford to give their wives such a lavish anniversary gift. And he still had another huge surprise in store.

The second the car ground to a halt, Susie launched herself into Elias's arms, unfazed by the center console digging into her hip. "This is too much!" Peeling herself away from his embrace, Susie's eyes welled with tears. "You've really outdone yourself."

"You deserve it, babe. A home away from home. We've been blessed. With the company running so smoothly now, I thought we should have a special place to get away, focus on each other, and unplug from all our responsibilities once in a while." Elias gently wiped some tears from Susie's cheek. They kissed.

"I love you," Susie said, her chin quivering slightly. "Now take me inside and show me the bedroom. I have a gift for *you*."

***

Afterward, Elias and Susie, sheened with sweat, lay with legs entwined in the white-walled bedroom. Outside the floor-to-ceiling windows, a few massive evergreens framed the lake's expanse. Fog fell from distant hills and rolled across the water.

"It's so beautiful. Peaceful," Susie said.

"The closest house is on the other side of the lake. We have our own private dock, private beach ..."

"Skinny dipping, nude sunbathing, sandy sex ..."

"Whatever you wish, beautiful."

"Gosh, we really needed this, didn't we? Our lives have been so hectic."

"I know. Sometimes I can't believe all that has happened. How my tinkering turned into what it has."

Susie loved her husband's humility despite all he'd accomplished in the decade since graduating college. He was a brilliant engineer, and his designs had revolutionized cellular technology. Yet, despite becoming wealthy, Elias regretted how much time he'd been away from his wife by burning the midnight oil, and he longed to adequately express how vital her support had been to him during the journey.

"You are a giant nerd, but a sexy one," Susie said.

Elias stroked Susie's auburn hair, kissed her bare shoulder as they spooned, gazing out the window. "I love you, and I'd be nothing without you."

Susie began shifting, pushing back into him. "You know ... spooning may lead to forking ..."

Elias chuckled. "Yes. Yes, it may."

Feeling like newlyweds and trying to remember the last time they'd gone twice in one day, the couple dressed, and Elias led Susie through all eight rooms of the lake house. She marveled at the sparse but stylish decor, mentally noting the minor additions and personalizations she'd like to make. Once the inside tour was complete, Elias led his glowing wife to the patio. The sun dipped behind the westering hills, the foggy light of the day readying to take a bow and exit stage left.

"There's one more part of the grounds I want you to see before it gets dark," Elias said. He directed Susie's attention toward a small building hidden from view from the front of the house and bedroom window.

"A little church? *What?*" Susie squealed with excitement. "It's so stinkin' cute!" Susie loved tiny things, and though not particularly religious, she was often filled with nostalgia remembering the Methodist community of her childhood. "How did you find this place?"

Elias fiddled with something in his pocket. "The realtor found it, not sure how. Apparently, the previous owner just took off, basically disappeared—some lay preacher with family money, I believe. The property went into foreclosure, and, well, here we are. Want to go see the church?"

Susie nodded enthusiastically and grabbed Elias's hand. They descended the porch steps and hit the path. The church, limestone-walled like the house, was roofed in oily black shingles and a cross-adorned steeple spiring high into the sky. Soon, Elias and Susie stood before the church's front doors, all dark and polished wood. Elias swung them open, flipped a light switch, and hung back at the entryway while a wide-eyed Susie walked past a few rows of wooden pews, reveling at the rustic appeal.

Before Susie turned back around, Elias withdrew his hand from his pocket and dropped to one knee between the pews. Susie spun, lips quivering as she saw the diamond ring between her husband's extended fingers—the one he'd promised eleven and a half years ago when he'd proposed with a synthetic diamond, all he could afford at the time. Susie had never complained; in fact, she still wore her ring proudly and had never once petitioned for a replacement despite all the success that had come in recent years.

"The past decade has been the best years of my life, and I'd like to officially renew our forever-vows. If you'll have me ..."

Susie burst into tears. "Yes! Yes! Of course! Yes!" She flung herself into Elias as he quickly stood.

Elias took Susie's hand, removed the old wedding ring, and replaced it with the new. "I have a pastor coming tomorrow at sunset. There's a boutique an hour from here with some items on hold for the ceremony. They're expecting us in the morning. And I have a photographer on standby."

"It's … perfect. *You're* perfect." Susie admired the diamond on her finger, pulled Elias tight, and began sobbing into his neck, eyes clenched tight. Their lives had diverted from the path they'd expected—their shared desire to have a family thwarted by both Elias's low sperm count and Susie's endometriosis—but they had a magnificent decade of marriage behind them, and both believed the best was yet to come. Hell, neither of them was even thirty-five. Their whole lives were ahead of them.

When Susie opened her eyes moments later, she nearly burst Elias's eardrum with a horrifying scream. Atop the back row of pews were two terrifying and incomprehensible creatures, their stubby, snake-like bodies black as tar, adorned with scaly, claw-laden arms and topped with maniacal rodent heads set with piercing, ruby eyes.

Elias released Susie, accidentally dropping her old ring to the floor. "What? What is it?" he said, spinning around to see the source of Susie's ill-timed fright. He saw a single obscure shadow slide into the church's dim corner, and his surge of adrenaline began to subside. "It was just a rat or something, babe."

Sputtering, shaking, Susie shook her head. "No. No-no-no-no … not *just* a rat, something else …"

"Let's go back to the house. Come on. I'll have an exterminator come in the morning. We'll have drinks and dinner …" Susie was out the door and halfway to the house before Elias could finish the sentence. What should have been a memory to last a lifetime was now run through with a rusty dagger. Elias began kicking himself for not thinking to have pest control come out before their arrival.

Elias sighed and began scanning the ground for Susie's old ring. He got on hands and knees and crawled down the aisle, searching under the pews. A glint caught his eye under the second row. He stood, walked forward, and leaned under the bench to retrieve the ring. As his fingers closed around it, he saw two beady sparks of red peeping around the pew's shadowed corner. It was a rat, all right. He leaped to his feet and bounded to the end of the bench, ready to stomp out the vermin's life. Instead of a scurrying rat, Elias saw something shiny and black slither into a hole in the corner. It appeared to be a thick snake tail capped with large sharp forceps, like those on the butt of an earwig but as long as human fingers.

A chill cascaded over Elias, and in seconds, he'd closed up the church and power walked back to the lake house. Susie stood over the kitchen island, sipping at an ice-filled glass of what looked like pure vodka, the drink jingling in her shaking hand.

Elias gave Susie a solemn, "Hey" and slid beside her, placing a hand at the small of her back. "You okay?"

"What were those things, Elias?" Susie said, gazing into her drink with glassed eyes.

Still grappling with his own sighting, Elias's mind churned for an answer. "I don't know, honey. We're right on the water, so probably some kind of water rat, a nutria, or something." Elias imagined the pincers and serpentine form had been simply a play of light and shadow. Memories were funny like that: malleable, mercurial, able to mold and shift to meet a need. Elias hoped they could return to the magical moment they'd been having.

Susie's glass clinked upon the marble counter, and she turned to face her husband head-on, her green eyes incredulous. "They had *scales.*"

"The lighting isn't great in there, babe. Their coats were just wet. Oil slicked. Look, either way"—Elias glanced at his watch—"I'll call for pest control first thing in the morning, and I'll get someone out here to patch that hole in the baseboard. Whatever it is, I promise the problem will be solved before our ceremony tomorrow. Okay?" He gently took Susie's hand.

She took another quick sip of her drink before meeting his gaze. "Okay. It just really scared me. I'm sorry, I know I ruined the moment—it would have been so perfect."

"We'll be laughing about it by tomorrow. This is just the beginning of what will be a magical week." As Elias finished his statement, a saying flashed in his mind: *We plan. God laughs.* He pushed it away. Taking Susie's other hand, Elias playfully swung her arms back and forth, determined to free a smile from behind her cold shell of nerves.

The corners of her lips rose, a shimmer of light returning to her eyes. "All right." She glanced at the diamond just beyond Elias's fingertips. "The ring is gorgeous. How did you know I wanted to renew my vows?"

"I halfff my wayzzz," Elias said in a mock Dracula voice, and Susie squeaked a mousy laugh. "Now," Elias said, "the fridge and pantry should be stocked. Why don't you poke around and decide what you want me to make for dinner while I unload the car?" He took a sip from Susie's glass and grimaced. "I wouldn't mind a drink, perhaps with some lime and soda."

"Okay, husband." Susie smiled, the scales of her fear sloughing away.

"And music!" Elias whipped out his phone, connected to the Sonos system he'd had installed, and opened his Spotify account. "You pick," he said, handing over his phone. He kissed Susie and exited the room.

When Elias reentered the lake house with their suitcases, the rhythmic guitar melody of Leon Bridges's "River" suffused the house with warmth, successfully dispelling the dark mood.

Elias felt much better while enjoying his second drink and sprinkling rosemary on chicken quarters to slide under the broiler. The memories of the ominous creatures had safely slid behind the walls into the crawl space of his mind.

***

The lake house was full of unfamiliar noises in the night, and the moonlight filtering through layers of crawling fog cast the bedroom in spectral shadows and dancing, jittering shapes reminiscent of the unidentified creatures in the church. Elias slept restlessly despite drinking too much vodka, and after awakening at dawn in a cold sweat, he opted to keep his ill-omened dreams to himself.

In his particular nightmare, Susie had begun coughing and choking at the precise moment she was to recite her vows. Her eyes had gone wide, her face red as she clawed at a throat corded and lined with bulging veins. One of the terrible black creatures then burst from her mouth in a violent spray of blood, and she fell to her knees. More creatures clawed their way out from behind her eyes and ears, flinging gobbets of flesh upon Elias's pressed gray suit. The white of Susie's dress then went red at her crotch, the wild protrusion pushing at the inner wall of her dress all too reminiscent of the inaugural chest-bursting scene from the movie, *Alien.* In the background, a sallow-faced reverend filled the small church with cackling, sinister laughter. As Elias's own throat swelled with a vile blockage, he had awoken, gasping for breath.

The fog had lifted; the lake faintly glistened with echoes of the rising sun. Elias appraised his wife, enjoyed the susurrus of her sleeping breath for a moment, then quietly rose from the bed and closed the bathroom door behind him. After splashing cool water on his face and toweling off his damp extremities, Elias went to the kitchen and made a pot of coffee. His cell phone rang at 8 a.m. sharp, and Elias slid out to the back porch to field the call from the exterminator, thrilled that his late-night text and email offering double pay for an early morning appointment had had the desired effect. Delbert McCormick, the deep-voiced man whom Elias imagined weighed well over three hundred pounds, had even offered to patch up any holes he found that gave the critters a pathway in and out of the building, and Elias was glad to check one more thing off the list. He reentered the house as Susie sauntered into the kitchen with tousled hair and sleepy eyes.

"Morning, bebe," Elias said. "How'd you sleep?"

"Could've been better." Susie poured a cup of coffee and went to the fridge for milk. "Too much vodka last night."

Elias scanned Susie's face as she stirred her coffee, hoping she hadn't been afflicted with frightening dreams as he had. Susie took a sip, gave a satisfied "ahh," and kissed Elias on his stubbled cheek before sitting beside him at the kitchen table.

"So, that *one* matter is taken care of; the exterminator will be here in an hour, and we don't need to wait around while he works," Elias said. Susie gave him a quick look as if she'd forgotten his promise to handle the gassing of critters inside the church but quickly refocused on her coffee. He continued, "I thought we'd have a small breakfast, then make our way to Estrella's Boutique, and then maybe have some lunch at the Casa Lago Winery before coming home. Sound good?"

"Mm-hmm. Sounds nice." Susie held her mug in both hands, determined to absorb every warmth her coffee offered.

"I also need to let the photographer know yay or nay. I didn't know if you'd want the extra body here or to keep it as private as possible. My little birdie told me you liked the idea of leaving families out of it this time. Hope that info was accurate."

"It is, and I'll have to thank Liz for conspiring to make this dream come true."

Elias laughed. "She did order me to have professional pictures taken, but I wanted to leave that part up to you."

"I think it would be nice to skip that part, too. I don't want anything to take the focus off of you and our little magic moment with the pastor. He can surely snap some photos for us with our phones."

"God. I love you—so low maintenance. I'll text her now. I'm sure she'll be happy with the deposit I gave her to keep the time open."

"My little planner. Always thinking of everything." Susie patted his hand.

"There is one last thing I couldn't plan for without spoiling the surprise: I wrote my own vows this time. Is it too short notice for you to write some, too? Maybe you could slip off somewhere quiet while I make—"

"Baby, I've had vows written for a renewal ceremony since the month after our fourth anniversary, and I've revised it every year."

Elias figured as much, especially after speaking with his sister-in-law. Still, knowing that his wife had prepared for the past six years created a tsunami of love and gratitude upon his soul. They'd had some rough patches, especially the insurmountable sadness at not being able to conceive, but overall, Elias felt unduly blessed in his relationship, and at times, even unworthy of such a perfect spouse. "You are *fucking* amazing."

"I know," Susie replied and playfully flung her hair over her shoulder, fluttering her eyelashes and pouting her lips.

An hour later, the happy couple narrowly edged their car by the exterminator's orange truck on the gravel drive, and Elias waved, noting that he'd been correct in his belief that Delbert was a large man. Elias hoped he was adequately prepared.

On their earlier call, Elias had said, "Mr. McCormick, I'm afraid I can't tell you exactly what our little church is infested with. I don't care if you find spiders, snakes, rats, or goddamned Keebler elves in that little church, just kill 'em all and leave no evidence."

Delbert had laughed a jolly laugh and replied, "You got it, Mr. Pechman. No worries. I'll have it cleared out, cleaned up, and ready for you and the missus before y'all are back from town. I'd just stay clear 'til noon so it can air out. I'll email you an invoice when I'm done."

When Elias and Susie Pechman returned to the lake house a little before 2 p.m., Elias had yet to receive anything, but Delbert McCormick and his bright orange truck were nowhere to be found.

***

Delbert McCormick's friends called him "Del"—the few friends he had that could speak, anyway. Considering his line of work, many would find his collection of pets quite peculiar; his home was brimming with aquariums and enclosures containing all manner of insects, reptiles, and rodents—all named—and the harmless ones were handled regularly. Del's favorites were two Mexican redleg tarantulas, Arachne and Uttu, an emperor scorpion named Serket, and a reticulated python he affectionately referred to as Indy's Nemesis. While he owned a half dozen rodents, his R.O.U.S., "Rousey," or "Ronda Rousey" (Del giggled every time he used this name), a marvelously fat, brown rat, was the centerpiece of his collection. Rousey spent most evenings on Del's lap or shoulder in front of the TV, sharing any manner of snacks, most often crunchy Cheetos. Delbert McCormick was what many would refer to as an "odd bird," to say the least.

Parking his truck in front of the Pechmans' small church, Del slid his heft out of the cab and began gathering supplies. With the couple gone, Del could capture any desired specimens to add to his collection without the fear of scrutiny. He had acquired many of his pets this way, and whenever possible, he practiced catch and release instead of extermination. Most of his customers would likely disagree with this practice, but pest control was not a business where your clientele desired to peek over your shoulder while you worked.

Del's first order of business was a thorough inspection of the premises followed by an attempt to capture as many of the undesirables as possible before donning his executioner's mask and gassing the place to high heaven. He switched on an air compressor mounted on the back of his truck and began unwinding the hose so he wouldn't get snagged or tangled when he was ready to use it. He slid on thick, elbow-length gloves to protect him from bites, stings, or claws, should he need to use his hands to guide whatever awaited him into his traps.

Though content with his own meager living, Del took a moment to appreciate the massive lake house and its picturesque setting from his vantage point before the church. The sun shone warmly on his neck. The smooth stretch of the lake was but a mirror reflecting the cotton ball clouds, the verdant hilltops, and the orange ball of fire moving steadily toward its peak in the sky. Del eyed the distance to the water and began mentally cataloging what he might find inside the church, curious as to why the pests wouldn't have nested in the big house, too. Del thought they hadn't seen each other yet. He'd be happy to come out again once they did.

As Del swung open the church's double doors, he took a deep breath, and, in his booming John Goodman voice, gave his petition to the seemingly empty space. "Show me your secrets, little church." Then, thinking the location would make it an appropriate addition, added, "There is nothing hidden that should not be made manifest ..." He laughed at himself and his flair for the dramatic, treating the Bible verse as though it came from some dusty grimoire.

The church's interior had a peculiar smell Del couldn't identify—something reminiscent of stagnant water and exotic spice—and not much light made it through the small windows set in the westward wall. Finding the light from the soft yellow bulbs insufficient for his task, Del slid a flashlight from his belt and began inspecting the church's nooks and crannies, quickly finding a softball-sized hole in the northeast corner where the unnamed critter escaped the wrath of Elias's boot heel. Del found identical holes in all of the church's corners, and their uniformity made him certain they were put there by the builder. "Odd," Del muttered.

Odder still, he found the church devoid of cobwebs and dust—not even a dead fly in a windowsill, a scattering of tic-tac turds, or a single silverfish frozen in supplication under a pew.

Del exited the church and began inspecting the exterior.

In most cases, it was easy to identify cracks and crevices in the foundation where vermin found entry, yet Del was at a loss. The only thing noteworthy was the ancient-looking stones lining the base of the structure; they were only visible around the church's backside and hidden behind a low-standing line of shrubbery. To Del, it appeared as though the small church was built upon something much, much older, but he knew zip about construction.

Increasingly confounded by the task before him, Del returned to his truck and gathered three additional containers to place by the strange, uniform holes in the church's corners. He would use duct tape and small pieces of flexible dryer vent hose to make an inescapable path between the holes and traps, and then blast compressed air into the remaining opening. This almost always drove anything hidden in the walls out into the open, and Del could simply move from hole to hole, replacing his traps, until he'd cleared the crawl space—it had worked many times before. In fact, it was how he came to own Ronda Rousey. Still, he usually had to make these holes himself; something was unsettling about the ready-made holes' uniform placement.

With one trap under each arm and one in each hand, and the vent hoses already secured over the trap door openings, Del approached the church's front doors. Clouds had rolled in during his inspection, and now the church's inner sanctum was murky, veiled from the light. His attention fell upon the hose attached to the trap in his left hand as he mounted the steps, and, crossing the threshold, his grip slipped, the trap clattering to the floor and the hose fully detaching. Del grumbled, knelt just inside the doors, and set down his remaining contraptions while he recovered the one he'd dropped. His mouth went dry, and suddenly, the church was filled with a synchronous chittering in full stereo sound. Del looked up to see the tops of all the pews and the small pulpit lined with black creatures unlike he'd ever seen, their red eyes locked on his. Their thick, serpentine tails were curled underneath their amorphous faces with long, dull pincers clacking together rapidly like a crowd of clapping, dead-faced spectators.

Del shrieked, dropped his trap, and leaped to his feet, knees popping. Two creatures launched from their positions above the door frame, their clawed appendages digging into Del's shoulders as their stubbed tails flung around and their pincers clasped on either side of the fat man's fleshy throat. Del went silent midscream and stood upright, his eyes grayed, his expression slack. The black things, their tail forceps squeezing tight, whispered an unbroken sibilance into his ears.

Del gathered all of his belongings—his traps, the uncoiled compressor hose—in smooth yet mechanical movements and threw them in the bed of his truck. Under the hissing tutelage of his shoulder-mounted masters, Del clambered into his vehicle, fired it up, and slowly began driving between the trees beyond the church. It was a walking path, steadily rising to a cliff at the edge of the Pechmans' property, and Del's bright orange truck barely fit. The previously sunny day had turned grayscale, the sun fully shrouded in clouds, the lake's surface dull like paint primer. Del inched to the edge of the cliff, rolled down the driver's window, placed the vehicle in park, and exited onto the wind-worn rock. Both creatures' grip tightened, and Del quickly grabbed a large rock from the edge of the trail, placed it on the accelerator, and jammed the truck into drive, leaping back with agility previously unknown. The truck smashed into the surface of the water one hundred feet below. As it began to burble below the surface, Del turned onto the trail.

The black-skinned, red-eyed things continued to instruct from their shoulder perch (Ronda Rousey would have been jealous—if a rat could feel such a thing), and soon, Del crossed the threshold of the small church once again, his chin fanged in drool, brow laced in sweat. The remaining monstrosities faced the pulpit, and their chittering swelled as Del sauntered down the aisle, oddly glancing at the vile crowd like a bride on her wedding day.

The floor surrendered a faint *clunk* as Del's heavy footfalls reached the carpet behind the pulpit, and he quickly fell to the ground and flung the rug away, revealing a large trap door. The door creaked open, and as Del McCormick gazed with dead eyes into the pit's black depths, the two creatures upon his shoulder tightened their grip. His face hovered over the void. Drool fell from his mouth, but there was no *plunk* of saliva hitting the surface of still water far below. Then, lighting fast, Del's companions withdrew their pincers and plunged the sharp gunmetal tips into his throat, quickly lunging off the man's shoulders.

As Delbert McCormick fell forward into the abyss, his carotid arteries released in a magnificent spray. The congregation of chattering creatures yawned their razor-toothed mouths wide and sang in celebratory praise—a song like a chorus of cicadas on a sweltering summer evening.

The buzzing and thrumming melody continued on. Sometime later, a new form emerged from the pit sheened in a thick, black liquid, and the abysmal assembly rushed upon it like a pack of eager puppies. Their master had returned, still weakened, but with fire in his eyes.

With long flickering tongues, the swarm of creatures cleansed their master of the black oil, revealing a frail body lined with deep wrinkles. The old man withdrew a case from a compartment hidden underneath the pulpit and donned the dark clothes within, inserting a set of dentures to conceal a mouth of sharp, jagged teeth. Ready to reenter the world, the man set about his business—there was to be a ceremony within his church later today, and a substitution of officiants was needed.

***

After a tasting flight and a bottle of Viognier with lunch, Elias and Susie returned to the lake house buzzed and giddy. The sun shone again, the lake a radiant scene, yet clouds loomed over the hills on the far side of the water.

Susie had chosen a billowy white sundress and accompanying headpiece of white carnations and lavender for the ceremony; Elias, a heather gray linen suit over a white cotton shirt, no tie. They had three hours to kill until the pastor arrived, and Susie, feeling particularly amorous, was determined to spend a solid hour of that time in bed.

Elias parked, and as the dust drifted by, Susie leaned in and sucked her man's earlobe. Susie's hand found its mark, and she quickly confirmed her breath and tongue in Elias's ear had the desired effect. "Unwrap and hang our new clothes while I freshen up? Meet you in bed in five?"

Susie withdrew her hand, grabbed the house key, and hopped out of the car. Elias exhaled sharply and smiled as he watched his wife almost skip to the front door, thinking how reminiscent the recent moments had been to their courtship years ago—nothing was like falling in love. He repositioned his swollen member, eager to join his bride, and exited the car.

Moments after unpacking and hanging their ceremonial garb on coat hangers by the front door, Elias's phone rang.

"Mr. Pechman?" The voice was unfamiliar; the caller sounded elderly.

"Yes, this is Elias Pechman."

"Hello, Mr. Pechman, this is Adrian Teufel—*Reverend* Adrian Teufel—and I am calling because I am afraid I have some bad news."

Elias's heart took a quick plunge off the deep end.

"Pastor Forsythe has fallen terribly ill, and I understand he is scheduled to perform your vow-renewal ceremony in a few hours."

"Oh, no. Will he be okay?" Elias interrupted. The part of his mind not fearful of the ceremony's postponement tried to place Reverend Teufel's accent. He thought perhaps it was European, or possibly even German.

"I am not a medical man, so I cannot be sure, but it appears quite serious."

"Oh," Elias replied curtly, unsure what else to say.

"But do not fret; I can come in his stead, if that is acceptable. I have reviewed Pastor Forsythe's notes and assure you that I am more than capable of making the event ... *unforgettable.*"

A peculiar feeling passed over Elias, yet he quickly brushed it aside. "That would be wonderful, Mr.—Reverend Teufel. Thank you for notifying me and for being willing to stand in. Please do give Pastor Forsythe my best wishes for a speedy recovery."

"It is my pleasure, Mr. Pechman, and I certainly will. I will see you at *Die Schwarze Kirche* at 5 p.m. Goodbye."

The line went dead, and Elias pulled the phone from his ear and stared at it briefly. "*Schwarze Kirche?*" he muttered confusedly. Further thoughts were interrupted by Susie's plea from down the hall.

"*Baaabbbyyyy?* If you don't get in here and *fuck* me, I'll go crazy!"

Elias set his phone on the counter and began undressing as he made his way down the hall, instantly deciding there was no reason to tell Susie about the change. Considering she'd never met Pastor Forsythe, she wouldn't know the difference.

While Susie showered, dressed, and primped for the ceremony, Elias slipped outside and made his way down to the church to inspect the exterminator's work and ensure the florist had completed the final preparations after his departure. All of the clouds had fled the lake's surrounding hills, and the sun had ratcheted down in the sky. It would be a gorgeous view from the church windows, and Elias warmed at the thought of enjoying the sunset from the back porch after the ceremony. Susie would look beautiful in her wreath of flowers and flowing dress in the warm glow of the setting sun.

He flung open the church's heavy doors, astonished not even the faintest chemical odor wafted out from the building. Everything was pristine, and elaborate floral arrangements stood throughout the church in aromatic bouquets of white, pink, and lavender. Glancing toward the corner where he'd seen the creature he desperately wanted to believe was a water rat, Elias was pleased to find no discernible hole. He made a circuit of the small building to ensure all was in order and frowned as he stepped upon the dark carpet behind the pulpit and heard a muffled *clunk*. He would have to see to the loose board later.

Elias returned to the house, poured a short Scotch, and reclined in a chaise lounge by the bedroom window, enjoying both a view of Susie's backside in lacy lingerie and the glittering lake. Susie's tush got more attention.

Thirty minutes later, Elias dressed, gave himself a once-over in the mirror Susie still utilized, and, after getting an approving pinch on the butt from his bride, made his way to the living room to await Reverend Teufel.

A quick rap at the door came at 5 p.m. sharp, and Elias got a flash of nerves, not unlike on their wedding day when he'd feared locking his knees and passing out. Noticing the bottle of Balvenie on the kitchen counter as he made his way to the front door, he wished he'd had one more drink. Elias opened the front door to find a frail man dressed in all black, his head brightly covered in a shock of thin, white hair.

"Reverend Teufel, I presume?"

"Ah, Mr. Pechman, so wonderful to meet you!" The man, well into his golden years, extended a pale hand; Elias found himself impressed by the man's firm handshake.

Reverend Teufel's smile was full of brilliantly white Chiclet teeth. Dentures, Elias presumed. His dark, bagged eyes glimmered with youthful curiosity, and despite his sallow complexion and deeply lined face, Elias warmed to him instantly—the man had a palpable personal magnetism. "Nice to meet you, Reverend. Susie is still getting ready. Shall I show you the lay of the land while she completes her ritual before the magic mirror?"

Chuckling, he replied, "Yes, yes, of course. Lead the way, young l ad."

Elias closed the front door and led Reverend Teufel to a limestone path at the drive's edge. It wound between a small grove of blue spruce and united with the path leading to the back porch about a hundred yards from the building the man had referred to as *"Die Schwarze Kirche."* Elias's curiosity got the best of him as they approached. "Reverend, I'm curious. I believe you referred to our little church as something-*kuh-sha?*"

Reverend Teufel, still smiling, said, *"Die Kleine Kirche,* German for 'the small church.'" Telling Elias he'd referred to the building as *The Black Church* would certainly not help matters. "My apologies for not elaborating before; I was quite *close* with your property's former owner, and that was what he called your quaint sanctum. Actually, I performed the benediction at its completion."

"Oh. Wow," Elias replied. "I haven't gleaned any details about the previous owner. I just heard he was a preacher and had disappeared."

"He was a marvelous specimen in his youth, yet our line of work can become taxing. I'm afraid I have no other details to divulge."

Elias swung open the heavy doors, disappointed the Reverend had no additional information. He chose to swallow the other question on the tip of his tongue; besides, if the frightful amalgamation of creatures he and Susie had thought they'd seen had been real, he was certain the exterminator would have called him or said something.

After exchanging more pleasantries and discussing the game plan for their private ceremony, Elias connected a Bluetooth speaker to his phone and showed the reverend how to stop and start their two-song playlist, somewhat amused they had an entry and exit song planned for an audience of one. The reverend opted to stay in The Little Church "for a final review of his notes" while Elias reread his vows and retrieved Susie.

Susie was breathtaking, and Elias's heart fluttered at her sight; there was something magical about seeing your wife in all white that reinforced the idea of her being heaven-sent, pure, virginal. Elias felt as lucky as he had on their wedding day. As they strode down the limestone path toward the church, they removed and exchanged their wedding rings.

Elias and Susie passed through the open church doors, and Reverend Teufel started the music. Susie began to tear up as she discerned the song that she'd repeatedly said rang a chord of truth within her heart: "My Best Friend" by Tim McGraw. They entered the church and split, slowly gliding down the opposing aisles, each glancing at their best friend with misty eyes until they met in the middle. Reverend Teufel gave a warm greeting, a brief blessing, and then invited Elias to read his vows.

Pulling a slip of paper from his breast pocket, Elias began. "I'll never forget when I first laid eyes upon you in Philosophy 101, playing with your pen and meeting my gaze behind your square lenses. How you had that little line of ink high on your cheek like a blue eyelash when we first spoke. I'd mentally wished upon that eyelash, and it fluttered off my fingertip to the heavens, making my dreams come true. I thought I'd died when I first saw you on our wedding day three and a half years later. *You* were my first dream, and because of you, our life has become a fairy tale—not perfect, but full of magic. Your love has made me more than I ever thought I could be, and after ten years, I want nothing more than to continue to chase our dreams together, to continue making magic until we are old and gray. I love you, Susie Annalise Pechman, and I renew my vow to continue cherishing you, protecting you, and honoring you for the rest of our lives."

Tears dribbled down Susie's cheeks as Elias again slid the ring onto her finger, and Elias breathed deep, his mind flooded with blissful memories of their lives. Reverend Teufel gestured toward Susie as small panels opened in the church's rear corners; an audience began building upon the back of the pews. The Reverend's eyes went wide in approval, the couple so focused upon each other—and their peripheral vision shrouded with tears—that the movement went unnoticed.

Susie began off script with a soft laugh. "I was mortified when I saw that pen mark on my face after first meeting you, fearful something so small would make you not want to talk to me again, but our lives have grown beyond the superficialities of youth, into something deeper than I ever thought possible." She returned to her paper. "My life has changed beyond measure since we first met. Your patience, love, and kindness have given me a peace I didn't know possible, and your gentleness through our trials and tribulations held me together when I thought I'd fall apart. You have blessed my life in every way, fortified me with a belief in myself I thought I'd never have, created an all-pervasive joy running like a bright thread through the laughter *and* the tears. I want nothing more than to continue merging our lives together until the end of time. I love you, Elias Grant Pechman. Forever." Susie placed Elias's ring on his finger, and at Reverend Teufel's instruction, the couple leaned in, closed their eyes, and kissed like they were the only two people on the face of the earth.

Instead of playing "I'm Gonna Be" by The Proclaimers as instructed, Reverend Teufel tossed aside Elias's phone and spat out his shiny white dentures. Startled, Elias and Susie turned toward the sound. Abruptly, Reverend Teufel began a series of rapid gesticulations as two pairs of red-eyed creatures fell from their mounts on the church's high ceiling. Before their minds grasped the situation, jagged claws knifed into their shoulders as their throats were clenched from both sides by ice-cold talons. Elias and Susie's eyes bulged, then grayed over like those of a snake ready to shed its skin. The black things upon the couple's shoulders hissed their sibilant instructions as the *Thing* previously answering to the name Reverend Adrian Teufel began the actual ceremony he'd come to perform.

The pew-mounted creatures clacked their pincers, sang their eldritch cicada song as the Reverend of The Black Church—*The Devil of The Black Church*—continued his crazed gesticulations and accompanying guttural utterances. *"Deen-gotch ara eel toophay ... ara ile bara yegg ..."* He stepped from behind the pulpit, and three of his black minions clipped their pincers upon the rug and yanked it aside. The reverend raised his hands to the sky, his eyes now as black as the creatures' skin; the trap door rose, and a slick, oil-like substance began spilling out from the depths beneath the church, quickly flooding the entire floor.

The creatures tightened their grips around the Pechmans' throats, their inculcating hisses rising in volume as Susie and Elias began to disrobe. The black ooze pooled around their ankles.

The reverend switched to English. "By moving here, you have allowed my restoration, my resurrection, and in gratitude, I will grant you the singular longing of your hearts. In doing so, you will create the partner I've always desired, and allow my work to continue."

Elias and Susie now stood fully nude before the altar, and at the sibilant influence of the red-eyed monsters perched upon their shoulders, they laid together in the shallow black pool and intimately coupled for the final time.

"Eltchoo raga ... biern zelgu raga ... atya-atya-pelg-pelg!" The Devil of The Black Church yelled from the altar, a smoky helix swirling about him.

Elias's thrusts began to accelerate amidst the black soup, Susie releasing forced exhalations as Elias's weight pressed upon her diaphragm. Elias groaned in climax, and the beasts upon his shoulders released his lifeblood from the confines of his arteries, the spray raining upon the church's inner sea of black. He fell upon Susie and was quickly dragged off her writhing form by an army of the black creatures. Already, Susie's middle was swelling, inflating with new life.

The reverend wailed in laughter as Elias's body floated before him upon the black, shimmering ink. Simultaneously, the ooze began climbing the reverend's legs and swallowing Elias's corpse, and just before Elias's bloody face was covered, a jet-black stream shot from the reverend's too-wide maw, connecting him to Elias with a shuddering obsidian cable. Elias's form melted away into the blackness, and slowly his features, his likeness, began to emerge upon the being who'd answered to the name Adrian Teufel for a few short hours of the dying day.

The chorus of chittering creatures continued their song as Susie Pechman gave birth and a being identical to Elias Pechman—but for obsidian eyes—delivered what appeared to be a healthy baby girl. She released a single warbling wail and opened her eyelids to reveal glimmering black marbles. The things on Susie's shoulders created a crimson fountain from the new mother's neck before leaping away; the spray rained upon the silent newborn as the church's black sea began to engulf the lifeless form of Susie Pechman.

Over a few short minutes, the ghastly cicada song still thrumming in the background, Susie's form shrank into the ink as the body of the black-eyed baby grew and grew and grew. Every detail of Susie Pechman's appearance, from her flowing auburn hair to the teardrop birthmark upon her inner left thigh, soon emerged fully upon the rapidly maturing life nestled in the arms of the Elias-thing—The Devil of the Black Church.

Outside the church walls and across the lake, the sun prepared to fall below the hilltops. Inside the church, the inky sea withdrew into the depths beyond the trapdoor, and the congregation of creatures silently slid back into the walls as the male and female form dressed in the ceremonial attire that laid upon the front row of pews.

The new Elias and Susie Pechman, the blackness slowly fading from their eyes, exited the church and traversed the limestone path hand in hand. They mounted the porch steps, slid comfortably into the cushioned patio furniture, and together watched the sunset. As the day's light fully withdrew from the sky, The Devil of the Black Church turned to speak to his newly animated partner with a fresh voice: the voice of Elias Pechman. "Come inside, my bride. The Pechmans' resources are vast, and there is a huge world out there. Our supply of converts will be virtually endless ..."

Acknowledgements

June Visosky & Stephanie Vislay

Bringing this anthology to life has been a journey filled with creativity, collaboration, and unwavering support. First and foremost, I would like to extend my deepest gratitude to the talented writers whose words grace these pages.

A heartfelt thank you to my co-editor, Stephanie Vislay. Your keen editorial eye, dedication, and thoughtful insights have been instrumental in shaping this anthology. Your insights, patience, and tireless efforts have made this process not only rewarding, but also a true collaboration in every sense. I am deeply grateful to have had you by my side in this effort.

To those who granted permissions for previously published works, we appreciate your generosity in allowing us to share these pieces once more.

A special thanks to the cover designer, Predrag. Your creativity has added yet another layer of beauty and depth to this book.

Lastly, to our families, friends, and loved ones—thank you for your unwavering support, patience, and encouragement. Your belief in this project has been a source of strength throughout this process.

This anthology is a labor of love, and I am honored to share it with you.

With gratitude,
June

It has been a joy (and, at times, an exercise in controlled chaos) to bring together such unique voices for this collection. Every story in these pages adds something unexpected—secrets that unravel, shadows that stretch, and twists that, frankly, I wish I had thought of myself.

A special thank you to the authors I personally invited to be part of this. Your willingness to jump in and create something powerful means the world. And to those who put their trust in a small publisher still finding its footing—you have my deepest gratitude. Your belief in this project, in this vision, has made it what it is.

A huge shoutout to June, whose detail-oriented brilliance has saved this project more times than I can count. I don't know how she does it, but I'm just glad she does.

To Laura, my constant, unwavering supporter—you've been there through it all, and I can't thank you enough.

To the beta readers and early supporters, you brave souls who stepped into the darkness first and gave us invaluable feedback—you are the real MVPs. I hope the stories didn't mess with your sleep too much.

And to everyone who had a hand in this anthology—editors, designers, those who cheered from the sidelines—thank you. You made this book what it is, and I promise I only cursed under my breath a few times.

Finally, to the readers who dared to step into the darkness... I hope these stories pulled you in, kept you guessing, and stay with you long after you've turned the last page.

With appreciation and a touch of unease,

Stephanie

LAURA FOLEY

www.laurafoleyauthor.com

Laura Foley is an Irish author hailing from the Kilkenny Countryside where she grew up on a small dairy farm. She now lives on the coast of Wexford with her husband and three children.

With a BA (hons) in Applied Social Studies, she graduated top of her class in 2016. Although writing for four years at this point, after completing her thesis, she finally found the confidence to consider writing as a career.

Laura likes to write in every age category from picture book to adult. But specifically, she only writes stories centered on Irish characters and places. She also loves writing with lyrical tones and enjoys stories that take place within time or place constraints to amplify the emotions of both the characters and readers.

Fans of the female Irish literary scene will be drawn to her romance work.

ADAM BASSETT

www.adamcbassett.com

Adam Bassett (he/him) is a UX / UI designer, author, and illustrator currently based in Vermont.

He's the author of *Digital Extremities* and *Animus Paradox*. Other short fiction of his has been published in *Nature Erupts, Blooms of Dawn,* and select issues of *Worldbuilding Magazine.*

Bassett's maps have been published in books such as *Season of the Dragon* by Natalie Wright, *The Ascenditure* by Robyn Dabney, and *Under a Pirate Flag* by B.H. Pierce.

ROWAN WOLF

www.rowanwolfauthor.com

Rowan Wolf is a writer, publisher, and dedicated caffeine addict living in southern California with her family and two golden retrievers—her most loyal (and occasionally disruptive) coworkers. Originally from Ohio, she has a background in design, which mostly means she spends an unreasonable amount of time obsessing over fonts and rearranging things that were probably fine to begin with.

When she's not knee-deep in publishing (or trying to convince herself that one more spreadsheet will solve everything), she's lost in the world of her epic fantasy series, *Canen Dera*—a project that's been with her so long, it might as well start paying rent. She survives on an unholy amount of coffee in the morning, cabernet at night, and is even trying to step away from the desk, training to hike El Capitan in Yosemite, because, apparently, fresh air is important.

FREDRICK CHARLES MELANCON

Frederick Charles Melancon lives with his wife and daughter in Mississippi.

He writes poetry, fiction, and nonfiction, and more of his works can be found in places like *The Hooghly Review, Eye to the Telescope,* and *365tomorrows.*

C.W. STEVENSON

A native of San Antonio, Texas, C. W. "Clint" Stevenson resides there with his wife, sons, and their retinue of furry companions. In his spare time, he reads vigorously, spends time with his family, and collects too many books to read in one lifetime.

Clint's work can be found in dozens of magazines and anthologies, including Summer of *Sci-Fi & Fantasy Volume 4*, *Chthonic Matter Quarterly*, and *Monster Fight at the O.K. Corral Volume 1*.

E.S. RAYE

esraye.com

E. S. Raye was born in the Zeti Reticuli system and came to Earth as a young isopod with stars in his eyes. After quickly mastering the childlike dominant language of North America, he is now just showing off ...

Okay, not really. But the truth is far more mundane.

Now living in southern Ontario, Canada with his amazingly patient wife, two cats, one stubborn French bulldog, and a happy-go-lucky mutt from Greece, E. S. Raye is a reformed marketing and content writer that has decided to clean up his act and pursue his dream of making a living writing fiction.

To that end, he is the founder and Editor in Chief of *Perseid Prophecies Magazine* and writes mostly horror and science fiction screenplays, short stories, and novels, including his debut space-western *Gas Giant Gambit: A Tall Tale From Beyond the Cygnus Rift*, coming September 2025.

L.N. HUNTER

L. N. Hunter's comic fantasy novel, *The Feather and the Lamp* (Three Ravens Publishing), sits alongside works in anthologies such as *Best of British Science Fiction 2022* and *Ghostly*, as well as several issues of Short Édition's *Short Circuit* and the *Horrifying Tales of Wonder* podcast. There have also been papers in the *IEEE Transactions on Neural Networks*, which are probably somewhat less relevant and definitely less entertaining.

When not writing, L. N. occasionally masquerades as a software developer or can be found unwinding in a disorganised home in Carlisle, UK, along with two cats and a soulmate.

FARAZ REZAI

Faraz Rezai is a contemporary literature student at King's College London. He's been writing for many years now, focusing specifically on prosaic short fiction, and has won a number of online competitions.

"The Gravekeeper" is Faraz's first official publication. He is also currently working on his first novel, *A Path Between Heaven and Earth*, which is a fictitious reimagination of the Genesis story, and which he hopes to have completed by the end of 2025.

JULIA RYLEN

Award-winning author Julia Rylen grew up on the sandy beaches of southwest Florida. After living in the Wild, Wild West (specifically, Colorado) for more than twenty years, she traded in her snowboard for water skis and returned to her home state.

When she's not writing, you can find Julia sitting under a coconut palm, enjoying an unsweetened iced Jasmine tea with her nose in a book. She's always on the hunt for her next pair of over-the-top sunglasses, or a thrift store find so valuable, she can retire to the Maldives.

While she writes magical realism, fantasy, science fiction, and dystopian stories, Julia's favorites by far are fairy-tale retellings, especially ones featuring a round table and a certain knight in shining armor who is enamored by the queen.

RACHEL SHARPTON

Rachel Sharpton has been interested in the weird, wondrous, and fantastic ever since her mother first read the *Lord of the Rings* trilogy in its entirety out loud when she was eleven years old.

Hailing from Los Angeles, California, she pursued her MA in Creative Writing at Swansea University in Wales and now resides in The Netherlands. As a lover of languages, she is currently stumbling her way through Dutch, though she also speaks some Mandarin Chinese and Japanese.

A world traveler at heart, Rachel would also love to see Earth, our beautiful blue dot, from space one of these days.

ROSALIE A. PENG

Rosalie A. Peng is an Asian-Canadian author and graduate of McGill University and Georgetown University Law Center. She now lives in Washington, D.C., where she works as a lawyer.

When not working on her debut novel, Rosalie daydreams about running an animal rescue and sanctuary.

JASON HERRINGTON

Jason Herrington discovered a passion for writing after years of blogging. He spent the first decade of his life in Saudi Arabia and bounced between Texas, Arizona, California, and Colorado. Currently, he is back in Texas.

While he mostly writes horror, dark fantasy, and suspense, he'll write a more sentimental piece now and again. When not working on novels or longer stories, Jason posts photo-inspired fiction on Instagram and short stories on his website and enjoys time with his family.

You can find his social media pages and a handful of creepy short stories at jmherrington.com